ONE MORE TIME

FIREWEED HARBOR SERIES

J.H. CROIX

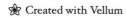 Created with Vellum

"Her heart did whisper that he had done it for her." ~Jane Austen

Sign up for my newsletter for information on new releases & get a FREE copy of one of my books!

http://jhcroixauthor.com/subscribe/

Follow me!
jhcroix@jhcroix.com
https://amazon.com/author/jhcroix
https://www.bookbub.com/authors/j-h-croix
https://www.facebook.com/jhcroix
https://www.instagram.com/jhcroix/

Chapter One

MCKENNA

What felt like hours upon hours after the wedding, I wandered through the main area of the ferry where we had the reception. It was summer in Alaska, so the sun had just set even though it was well past midnight. I stood in the room, spinning in a slow circle. Staff had swept away all evidence of the wedding, so the ferry would resume regular operations.

My heart pinched when my eyes snagged on a daisy that had fallen on the floor. I loved daisies, but they'd been ruined for me by my high school boyfriend.

Forget him.

I hated his name and didn't even like to think it. My one serious ex-boyfriend had left deep scars of cynicism in my heart when I'd learned the helpful lesson that some people wanted me for all the wrong reasons. He used to give me daisies.

"Whatever," I muttered to myself.

The newlyweds had retired to their honeymoon suite, one of the tiny cabins on the ferry. My brother Kenan insisted it would be romantic, even if it was crowded.

I shook my wistful thoughts away, focusing on how happy I was for my brother and Quinn. Nothing was better than best friends falling in true love.

With another spin, I walked out of the empty room. By the sounds coming from the cafeteria kitchen, I imagined they were prepping food for the following day.

I walked outside and saw the front deck, where a few people milled about the open area where tents were set up. The Alaska ferry system had options. There were actual cabins, a place to put up tents on the big deck, and a covered area with heat lamps where people claimed lounge chairs to sleep on in sleeping bags. Communal showers were available for those who didn't have their own cabins.

I stayed along the side deck where it was just me, accompanied by the sound of the ocean water lapping gently against the hull as the ferry moved through the dark waters of the Gulf of Alaska. When I rested my elbows on the railing, the metal felt cool against my skin. I took a slow breath, breathing in the crisp, briny air.

The sky was darkening to indigo with the barest hint of daylight left. I heard footsteps approaching and glanced to my side. My heart jolted as my eyes landed on the silhouette. I had looked at this man a few too many times this evening.

Jack Hamilton, the reason for my accidental black eye. I lifted my fingertips, lightly touching the flat of my cheekbone under my eye. It was puffy and a little sore.

"Hey, Jack Hamilton," I called over. A little splash in the water near the boat punctuated my voice.

A few long strides later, Jack stopped beside me. He had his hands stuffed in the pockets of his jeans.

"Hey, McKenna Cannon," he replied, his voice laced with a hint of humor.

"Nice wedding," he added after the moment began to stretch between us.

I tried to ignore the way my pulse kicked along faster and faster. "It was nice."

He stepped closer, stopping maybe only a foot away from me. I angled to face him slightly. He rested his hip against the railing, leaning an elbow on it. He studied me for a moment, his eyes lingering on my eye, the one that collided with the door he opened in the hallway hours and hours ago.

"How is your eye? It doesn't look too bad."

"Some good tricks with makeup help," I said dryly.

"I'm sorry," he offered.

"There's really no need to apologize. It doesn't hurt much. I was walking too fast and not paying attention. All you did was open the door. Maybe we should blame the ferry. Those hallways are narrow."

Jack's chuckle sent sparks scattering across the surface of my skin. Tingles spun in my belly.

"I'm glad it doesn't hurt too much," he added.

"It's a good story. Maybe we should go on a date so I can say you gave me a black eye when we met," I teased.

What in the ever-loving fuck?

I wasn't supposed to ask anyone out, much less this ridiculously hot man. My hormones' happiness at the sight of Jack was super inconvenient.

Jack was quiet for a beat. "Maybe we should."

For a few seconds that felt suspended, I trusted the look in Jack's eyes—the heat banked there, the intensity, and the encompassing focus on me.

But then, I remembered he knew my family. At least, now he did. So maybe I could ask him on a date, but surely, he would want something else. Not for me, but just because.

When your family has money, people think you're lucky. Maybe I didn't worry about paying the bills. That *was* a genuine blessing. But I had learned that when you have money, people want it. You never know if they want you for you or for your money and the connections it creates. I fervently wished for another few seconds that I hadn't met Jack under these circumstances. Because more than just a spark of chemistry burned between us. But I couldn't unwind time. I couldn't hope for a meeting where he didn't know who I was. Maybe I could think he just wanted me for me.

I took a shaky breath, forcing myself to shrug lightly, to play it oh-so-cool. "I was just kidding." My voice came out stilted.

Jack studied me for another moment, and anxiety tightened like a fist in my chest, making it hard to breathe for a minute.

I beat back the panic building inside, telling myself I could ignore it even though it was impossible. I'd had panic attacks since I was a little girl. Even though I didn't know that's what they officially were until I was in high school.

I didn't talk about them because I didn't want to. That was another secret I kept from my family. I hadn't had one in years, mostly because I did my best to avoid all triggers.

"I wasn't kidding," Jack finally said.

That got my attention. I peered up at him, cocking my head to the side.

"Really?" That single word was loaded with skepticism.

He didn't even look away as he nodded slowly. "Really."

"Oh." I chewed on the inside of my cheek.

Jack was quiet again before he angled his head, his gaze considering. "Is that such a surprise? You're beautiful, McKenna."

The sincerity in his voice brought tears to my eyes, startling me. I blinked quickly, looking away. What little light had been left lingering in the sky was gone now. The moon hung over the mountains, casting a crescent-shaped beam of light across the ocean, a shimmering blur on the dark surface.

I steeled myself. I was trying to find my footing in this conversation. I was used to feeling uncertain about men and doubting intentions. I acknowledged those doubts as facts, as easily as accepting that the sky was blue and that I needed air to breathe, water to drink, and food to eat. These were all facts of life.

I felt this surprising pull to Jack. I didn't want to use the word magnetic, but that was the only word that came to mind. When I trusted that the tears were safely banished, I glanced back toward Jack, shrugging. "I guess. Once people know who my family is, they usually want something from me. If I'm actually beautiful to you, that's a surprise." I was proud there wasn't even any bitterness in my voice.

Jack looked dismayed.

"Well, that fucking sucks," he said flatly after several beats of silence.

"It's just practical."

He looked away, out over the ocean. I could see the muscles in his jaw clenched tight. His shoulders rose when he took a deep breath. He let it out in a controlled sigh when he turned back toward me. "Do you think Quinn married your brother for his money?"

I shook my head before I could even think it through. My faith in Quinn's love for Kenan was unshakable. "Absolutely not."

"What about Haven and Rhys? And Blake and Fiona?"

"It seems like you know my whole family," I hedged, my tone sarcastic as I sidestepped his question.

"I met them all today," Jack said. "Everyone seemed pretty happy. It was nice to see."

"Fine," I muttered. "They're all happy. If you must know, I don't think any of their spouses chased them for money. I just haven't been that lucky."

He studied me while I ignored the way my belly felt all fluttery and tingly. Sweet hell. Just looking into his eyes made me feel like a teenage girl again. I wanted his approval. I wanted him to like me. I wanted him to kiss me and to mean it when he said I was beautiful. It's not that I doubted him specifically. It's just I didn't really believe it. It wasn't him. It was me.

"Because it bears repeating, you're beautiful, McKenna." At that, Jack stepped away from the railing.

"I'll see you when I see you," I called as he walked away.

Chapter Two

JACK

I curled my hand over the door handle, pausing for a second before I opened it. Ever since I opened a door directly into McKenna Cannon's face, I always gave it a second to make sure I didn't hear footsteps coming down the hallway.

In a few hours, the ferry would dock. With my move to Fireweed Harbor on the horizon, I was confident I would see McKenna again. Yet I wanted more than a few minutes of conversation with her before the end of this ferry trip.

I wanted a lot more than that. I wanted to kiss her senseless. I wanted to walk on a beach with her.

Lately, my parents said I was broody. That was how my mother described me ever since my engagement blew apart. Oh, it was nothing tragic. Just that my ex wanted children, and I didn't.

I had come to terms with that, but she hadn't. She said I should've been more upset about it. Of course, my mother didn't want to acknowledge why I might've been broody. My brother, also my best friend, was dying from cancer. I gave myself a mental shake, kicking those thoughts away.

Walking down the hallway, I lifted my gaze from the floor when I heard a door open ahead. McKenna stepped out but didn't even look up even though she walked swiftly toward me.

For a moment, I considered just letting her run into me. The hallway was narrow. After being responsible for opening the door she collided with, that didn't seem fair. The door situation had been a genuine accident.

"McKenna."

Her head whipped up, and her shoes scuffed on the carpet when she stopped abruptly.

"Jack!" she squeaked, her pretty silvery-blue eyes widening.

I stopped in front of her. "McKenna." My lips curled up at the corners.

She blinked up at me. "What are you doing?"

"Well, right this second, I'm walking to the cafeteria to get some coffee and breakfast before the ferry docks. You?"

McKenna peered around my shoulder and gave me a sheepish smile when she looked back at me. "I went the wrong way. I get turned around in here."

"Shall we go to breakfast together, then?"

She smiled and turned to walk beside me.

A full twenty minutes later, I realized my mistake. Spending time near McKenna created a drumbeat of need inside me.

All the while, I kept recalling her comment about people wanting her for her family's money. I recognized the flash of uncertainty flickering in her eyes and wanted her to forget that.

At some point, a few hours later, we docked at

Diamond Creek, Alaska. Cars rolled off the ferry, and I saw McKenna standing in the parking area. There was a man nearby. Her hand was curled around the hem of her shirt, her thumb and forefinger sliding back and forth nervously. I was waiting for my cousin to pick me up.

For different reasons, I felt drawn toward McKenna. I didn't like the uncertainty she exuded. I also didn't like how the man nearby looked at her. A woman stood with him, and her expression was tight, haughty almost.

When I stopped beside McKenna and her eyes met mine, I said, "Hey, sweetheart."

Her eyes widened slightly, but she went with it. "Hey." Her tone was a little forced, as was her smile. Fuck it, I was in this.

The man glanced back and forth between us curiously while the woman narrowed her eyes. "Who are you?" she asked as I slid my arm around McKenna's waist.

I gave them a cursory glance. "Jack Hamilton." I could feel the tension emanating from McKenna. I didn't know the details, but I knew this man had hurt her. He also sure as hell didn't like my presence.

"Who is McKenna to you? I've never seen you," the guy said.

"I don't see why that matters." With a glance down at McKenna, I slid my arm more fully around her waist and bent low. I meant to kiss her briefly in order to make some kind of point. Usually, I thought things through, but McKenna's presence and feeling her distress wiped any capacity for critical thought away.

The second my lips met hers, it was as if a lightning bolt had struck between us. Electricity sizzled through the air. Her lips were soft, and she let out a startled little gasp.

I needed more. I angled my head to the side and decided to make this count. When McKenna let out another sigh, her lips parted just enough for me to tease my tongue into her mouth, twining with hers as I stepped closer and slid my hand into her hair.

For the next moment, I forgot everything but her. She tasted sweet, a little bit like sugar. I could feel the soft give of her breasts as she arched up against me. I dove into our kiss, taking deep sips from her mouth before someone clearing their throat snapped into my awareness.

I lifted my head, opening my eyes to see McKenna's surprised, hazy gaze. "Nice to see you, sweetheart," I murmured.

"Well, that was a bit much," the woman said sharply.

I ignored her, holding McKenna's gaze. "Let's go." I turned to the side, keeping my arm firmly around her waist, and began to walk.

Chapter Three

MCKENNA

A few months later

An icy blast of wind gusted across the harbor. I stuffed my hands a little deeper into the pockets of my down jacket as I walked quickly down the street. The sign for Spill the Beans Café glittered on this gray winter day.

My lips curled in a smile as I turned up the walkway. I wished I had some beans to spill.

"No, you don't," I said to myself.

"Who are you talking to?" My older brother's voice reached me just as I walked through the doorway.

I had seven older brothers to choose from. Of course, Blake had to be the one to catch me talking to myself.

"Myself," I countered with a jaunty grin. The only way to deal with Blake's teasing was to play it off.

"In that case, no, you don't, what?"

"I wasn't talking to you," I countered pointedly.

"You *are* talking to me. Right now, in fact," he returned.

I shook my head with a bemused chuckle just as Blake's wife, Fiona, stopped at his side. She nudged him lightly in the ribs with her elbow. "Leave her alone," Fiona ordered.

Blake glanced down, his brows rising in a look of faux outrage. "Leave her alone? Why do you assume I'm bugging her?"

Fiona's eyes met mine with a knowing glint. She looked back at Blake. "Because I know you. You usually tease your siblings, especially McKenna."

Blake, the brother I'd thought would never fall for anyone, looked at Fiona with pure love. He shrugged easily and curled an arm around her shoulders. "You might have a point.

I burst out laughing. I was happy for them. I *really* was. But I hated the little sting I felt on the surface of my heart. I wanted everyone to be happy and find their person, yet I'd accepted the fact that I didn't think I would ever trust anyone again. I'd also concluded I didn't want children. While I certainly wasn't reconsidering having children, doubts had started to swirl regarding my faith in *not* having faith in anyone.

I'd been wishing for things ever since that stupid kiss from Jack Hamilton.

Stupid, stupid, stupid.

"Is everything okay?" Fiona prompted, her gaze concerned.

"Oh, of course," I said, injecting some forced cheerfulness into my tone. "I'm just preoccupied and haven't had my coffee yet today."

Blake's eyes widened. "You'd better get some fast."

He waved me by them, and I rolled my eyes as I approached the counter. There was a lull in the flow of customers although the café was busy. Despite being fairly early for a winter morning, most tables were occupied.

Just as Blake began to say something else, the door to the café opened. My friend Tessa came in, her eyes catching mine as she released the door behind her.

"Hey, Tessa," I greeted, just as the door pushed open again.

My pulse skyrocketed the second my eyes landed on the man walking through. Tessa immediately glanced over her shoulder.

Jack Hamilton walked into the café. He glanced to the side when Blake said, "Hey there, Jack."

Of course, Blake knew Jack. Jack had met my whole freaking family on the ferry trip. Time ticked by in slow motion as Jack's gaze arced toward where Blake stood near me just as Tessa stopped on my other side.

"Hi, Blake," Jack said. His eyes met mine briefly, and he dipped his chin. "And McKenna."

"Wow, McKenna," Tessa murmured under her breath at my shoulder. "Who's this hottie?" Heat flashed into my cheeks. "Well, well," she teased.

"Don't even start," I ground out through gritted teeth.

Jack crossed the café, stopping in front of us. A few snowflakes dusted his almost black hair, and the flush on his cheeks from the cold outside highlighted his blue eyes. They appeared impossibly blue.

I didn't realize I was staring at Jack until Tessa elbowed me hard in the side. "Ooof," I grunted under my breath.

Tessa waggled her brows, and I looked away. Blake was saying something to Jack. I swallowed, pasting on something I hoped looked like a polite smile.

"So you've officially moved here?" Blake asked.

Jack nodded. "I'm staying at a local B&B while I wait to close on my house. I need to find a short-term rental, though, because the B&B rates are pricey."

Before I could stop myself, I chimed in, "I can have our property manager give you a call."

Jack's eyes locked on mine, and I willed the heat to cool in my cheeks. I hoped I didn't look as flustered as I felt inside. If Blake picked up on it, the teasing would be relentless.

"Property manager?" Jack prompted.

"We own some properties around town, and Sandy will gladly let you know what's available for a short-term rental."

"I think the house Haven was staying in is open," Blake added.

"I only need a place for about six weeks. I'm scheduled to close in a month, but I'd like a cushion in case something delays it," Jack replied. "Any suggestions you have for rentals would be great."

"Here, let me give you Sandy's number. What's your number?" I was functioning on autopilot at this point.

Jack recited his number, and I typed it into my contacts. "I'll send her your contact info and let her know what you need. You can give her a call as well."

"That would be great."

Blake said something when the door to the café opened again, a blast of cold air swirling in as my least favorite person in town entered. Cory was with his new fiancée, who hated me even though I'd never done anything to her.

We were clustered in front of the counter. Blake glanced over, his eyes narrowing when they landed on Cory. Cory was my boyfriend in high school, and I thought I was in love with him. We broke up after I found out he was dating me to get an "in" with my family. I heard him joking about it in school one day. There was that, and then his more current shenanigans when he reported on his podcast just a few months ago about the legal issues for my grandfather, who was recently sentenced for embezzlement related to our family's business. He was big on saying he was "just asking questions." In this case, he asked why only our grandfather was charged. He wondered who else in the family might also be a criminal. Just thinking about it caused anger to simmer inside. Cory dreamed of making it big with his podcast, which mostly involved peddling gossip about small-town issues with whatever twist he thought might get him the most clicks.

I found comfort in reminding myself that at least I'd never done anything more than kiss the jerk in high school. I ignored the bile in my throat and beat back the sneaky sense of insecurity that rose whenever we crossed paths.

Even though his fiancée, Heather, hated me, I was thrilled he was engaged. Mostly because I hoped he would leave me the hell alone. Unfortunately, Heather was jealous of me. She was convinced I still had a thing for him, which was insane.

The last time I'd seen them was hours after Jack had kissed me. I hadn't said a word to them, then or now. I still didn't know what prompted Jack to kiss me.

I felt Blake's gaze as he shifted, turning to angle his shoulder and effectively blocking me from their view. I didn't need my brothers to protect me, but they still did. Of course, we collectively couldn't stand Cory, and Rhys had even pondered legal action after the stupid podcast episode.

"Have you had coffee yet?" Tessa asked.

"Nope. Let's get in line."

I looped my hand through her elbow, and Jack stepped toward the counter with us. Blake followed.

"Didn't Fiona feed you?" I teased lightly. Fiona was a ridiculously good cook and also the chef for Fireweed Winery, our family's restaurant.

Blake grinned. "I can always use more food."

We stopped at the counter, and I told myself Heather's eyes weren't burning a hole in my back. Tessa teased Blake about ordering donuts, and I forced out a laugh that sounded fake to my ears.

Jack glanced toward me. "Any more ferry weddings planned?"

My belly did a little shimmy as I shook my head. "Not much call for those. So, uh, when did you get to town?"

"Just this week."

"When do you start work?"

"Later this week."

Blake interjected. "You're up." He gestured me forward as he stepped to the side.

Phyllis was at the counter. She smiled at Tessa and me before her eyes landed on Jack. "Good morning. You must be new to town."

"This is Jack." I gestured to him. "He was on the ferry a couple of months ago when Quinn and Kenan got married. He's taking a position on the firefighter crew here in town."

Phyllis glanced at Jack, her eyes twinkling. "Town or hotshot?"

"Hotshot," Jack replied with a grin.

"You're starting in the middle of winter?"

Jack nodded. "By the time fire season starts in earnest, I'll be ready to roll."

"Welcome to Fireweed Harbor. I hope I see you often. We *are* the best coffee shop in town," Phyllis said.

Jack's return smile was warm. "I love good coffee, so I'm sure you'll see me often."

"What can I get you?" she prompted.

He skimmed the chalkboard. "I'll take the house coffee as long as it's strong."

"It's plenty strong." Phyllis shifted her attention to Tessa and me. "Your usual?"

"Always," Tessa replied, and I nodded.

"Anything to eat?"

Blake called over from where he waited nearby. "If you want sweet, I vote for the pear muffins. If you want savory, go for the ham or spinach pastries."

I sidled away while Jack ordered. I could still feel Heather's eyes pinned on me, but I ignored her. The hum of conversation carried on around me.

I loved my hometown. I really did. But sometimes I felt caught in a tiny net. For example, I wanted to be unknown right now, just someone ordering coffee and living a quiet life.

Being the youngest sibling in a well-known family, with all our secrets sprinkled through the gossip chain in this tiny town, wasn't fun. I ignored the sting to my pride when I saw a few gazes bounce from me to Cory. I felt so stupid for even dating him and wished the shadows of gossip didn't cast so long. I imagined no one would've even remembered, but he'd talked about how he'd dated me in high school when he did the whole piece on the legal troubles for my grandfather.

He played it off like he knew our family well, which was such bullshit. I tried to tell myself it was all in my head.

I had to resist the urge but refused to let my gaze drift to Jack again. He was handsome and *way* too distracting. I didn't need any distractions. My life all by itself distracted enough.

"You could at least apologize." I whipped my head around to find Heather standing there.

"Excuse me?"

"To Cory," she said, each word sharp.

So much for hoping it was all in my head. I was legitimately confused. "For what?"

Heather rolled her eyes, letting out a little snort. "For cheating."

"What?" I yelped.

Just then, Cory approached, sliding his arm around her waist with a proprietary air. "Let's go," he said.

I stared at him. "What the hell are you telling people?"

Tessa happened to hear the entire exchange. "You know, that's not the first time that rumor has circulated."

"That I cheated? On him? For fuck's sake, we're talking about high school." My voice rose several octaves.

Jack was right there. He glanced curiously from me to Tessa.

My jaw tightened. I didn't owe anyone any explanation, much less a man I barely knew.

Blake caught my eyes. "It's bullshit. He's just milking the situation because of his podcast."

OMG with the drama. I could not deal and felt tired all of a sudden. "I'm going to the office." Right then, Phyllis slid my coffee toward me.

I glanced at Jack. "Welcome to Fireweed Harbor."
I lifted my coffee and hurried outside.

Chapter Four

JACK

"What the hell was that about?" I asked Blake as McKenna left the café.

Her hair caught the cold wind as she walked through the doorway and spun in a little swirl around her shoulders.

Blake rolled his eyes when I glanced toward him. "A bunch of bullshit. McKenna's ex." His tone was low and laced with anger. "He has a podcast where he talks about local Alaska stories. Because Fireweed Industries is big enough to matter, he did a piece when our grandfather got convicted for embezzlement. He tried to spin it that he knew the family well because he dated her in high school. In high school, McKenna dumped him. She didn't cheat on him," he added pointedly.

I didn't need Blake to make that point. Maybe I didn't know her all that well yet, but I knew McKenna would never do anything like that. My eyes followed McKenna through the windows. I could see her turning off the pathway into the café and onto the sidewalk. I wanted to know so many things about her. I dragged my eyes away, catching Blake studying me.

"I can't imagine she would," I belatedly replied.

His gaze lingered on me for another moment. Just then, the door to the café opened, a blast of cold air coming through as a pretty woman walked in with a small child holding her hand. I thought I recognized her, most likely from the wedding on the ferry. When Blake glanced her way, anything he might've been thinking about me was clearly forgotten.

The little girl released the woman's hand, skipping through the café with a wide smile stretching across her face.

"Hey, Lia," Blake said, leaning down to lift her in his arms and give her a spin.

She giggled. "Hey! Mom said you would be here, and you are!"

Just as the woman stopped beside me, I recalled her name. "Hi, Fiona."

"Jack! Nice to see you." Her smile was warm.

Blake lowered the little girl to the floor, and she studied me curiously as he leaned over and pressed a lingering kiss on Fiona's cheek.

"I know you!" Lia announced.

Fiona and Blake looked down at her. "You met him on the ferry at Kenan's wedding," Blake pointed out.

Lia angled her head to the side as she examined me. "Oh. You're Jack."

I grinned. "I am." I reached down to shake the small hand she thrust toward me. "You remembered my name."

She shook my hand vigorously before releasing it with a flourish. "I'm Lia," she announced.

"Do you want something to eat?" Fiona asked her.

"Hot chocolate and an orange cranberry muffin," Lia replied instantly.

Fiona glanced at the register. Phyllis served the last person in line before them, then looked up. "I heard. Coming right up."

Blake slipped to the register to pay while Fiona turned her attention to me. "You're starting a firefighter position here, right?"

"Good memory."

"It's the middle of winter," Lia pointed out. "Are you like Uncle Wyatt and Uncle Griffin? They say fire season is in the summer."

Fiona interjected. "Those are Blake's younger brothers. They're twins and also hotshot firefighters on a crew up in Fairbanks."

With a nod, I glanced down at Lia. "Fire season *is* mostly in the summer. I'm starting to train here now so I'll be ready when summer gets here. The crews travel to other areas if needed."

Fiona's daughter nodded solemnly. "Last winter, Griffin went to California."

Blake returned to Fiona's side, hearing Lia's comment. "We keep hoping to get them to move back to Fireweed Harbor."

"My position isn't the only opening here. They have a few because they're expanding with a new hotshot crew that'll be based out of here," I offered.

"I'm leaning on both of them to work for the family. We'll see," he replied.

I'd heard about the Cannon family before I even took the position here. Fireweed Industries was a big deal company and not just in Alaska.

"What do you do for the business?" I asked politely.

"I run the winery and brewery. Not the restaurant

portion but production and distribution. We're scouting for a new lead brewer. Our current guy is moving to Juneau with his wife because they're having a baby and want to be closer to her family. I'm hoping I can convince Wyatt to take over. He loves that stuff. I'm also hoping someday we can convince Griffin to help Kenan. Kenan's kind of our catchall. He does whatever we need, and we need at least two more of him."

"I can imagine. Fireweed Industries is a major corporation."

"It is, but being here in Fireweed Harbor, it's family-oriented," Fiona chimed in.

"Fiona's the chef at the winery restaurant," Blake explained, his eyes warm as he smiled at her. "I'm not technically her boss."

Fiona's cheeks flushed slightly as she rolled her eyes. "You technically *are*."

Phyllis called over, "Hot chocolate and muffin are ready."

With that interruption, I departed with a wave. As I happened to be walking out, the man I now knew to be a total jerk was leaving with the woman who had confronted McKenna. I followed them out, unabashedly listening because they didn't notice me.

I couldn't hear what the woman said, but the guy said, "Just get over it, Heather." She let out an annoyed huff.

I shook my head to myself. What a fucking asshole. Protectiveness flashed through me. I could only imagine what it was like to be McKenna or anyone in a family such as theirs. You'd always be wondering who wanted you for you and who wanted you for superficial reasons.

Chapter Five

JACK

"Jack here," I answered the call.

"Hey, hey!" Gage Hamilton's voice came through the line, and a smile tugged at the corners of my lips.

"Hey, how are you doing?"

Gage was my cousin. He and his siblings were the reason I fell in love with Alaska. Gage had moved back to Alaska to renovate the family ski lodge and created a beacon of sorts for the extended family. After a few visits there, I'd been keeping my eye on positions as a hotshot up here.

"What's up?" I asked.

"Just checking to see how it's going now that you've moved to Fireweed Harbor."

"So far, so good. I'm under contract for a house and have a lead on a short-term rental to stay in until I close," I replied, thinking of McKenna's number burning like a hot coal in my phone. "I also found my favorite coffee shop in town."

Gage chuckled. "Coffee is more important than a place to live," he replied dryly.

"Everything okay in Diamond Creek?"

"Always. Just had a minute, so I thought I'd check in. You heard from Derek?"

The lightness I felt inside disappeared swiftly. "Not in the past week or so. I'll let you know if I hear from him."

"Please do. I tried calling the other day and haven't heard back." Gage's voice was somber.

"I'll keep you posted if I hear any updates. I promise." We ended the call, and I took a swallow of my coffee, stopping on the sidewalk to take a steadying breath.

My heart felt scraped whenever I thought about my brother right now. After another breath, I began walking again, taking in the town. The town was beautiful in the winter, nestled at the base of the mountains with snow-capped peaks rising in a circle around the harbor. A glacier glittered blue under the sun, striking sparks off the icy surface. The water was calm today, with ice floes drifting along the edges of the shoreline.

I turned toward the docks. A high-pitched eagle screech stood out amid the seagull calls. I followed the sound to see the eagle sweeping low, its talons out to scoop a fish out of the water. I watched as it landed on the shore and immediately tore into the fish.

I shook the gloom settling inside my thoughts away. I had to compartmentalize. Because there was literally nothing I could do about my brother.

Chapter Six

MCKENNA

"Excuse me?"

"Call for you. Something about a rental," Tish said through the phone speaker.

My sister-in-law Haven and I were working on some graphics for an upcoming event for the winery. Haven was deep into adjusting the graphics on her laptop as she sat across from me at the conference table.

"Is Sandy available?" I eyed the conference phone as if Tish could see me.

"No, she's out today. Remember? She has a doctor's appointment."

"Oh, that's right. I'll take it. Did you happen to get a name?"

"Of course I did," Tish said, her tone affronted.

Haven waggled her brows and grinned over at me. We liked teasing Rhys's wildly efficient and organized receptionist. She was amazing, and we all loved her.

"I didn't mean to imply that you wouldn't have," I quipped with a grin.

"It's Jack Hamilton. He said you gave him Sandy's number."

My cheeks heated. Haven's eyes widened when she happened to glance back up at that moment.

"Okay," I managed through a swallow. "Put him through."

"Just a sec," Tish replied.

I heard the click of that line just before the next call line began blinking. "Are you taking this one on speaker?" Haven teased.

I narrowed my eyes at her. "No." Lifting the receiver, I answered, "McKenna Cannon here."

"McKenna," Jack said, the low rumble of his voice sending a hot shiver down my spine. "I thought I was getting Sandy."

"Um, she happens to be out today. I'm guessing you're calling about the rental I mentioned."

"That I am. Should I wait until Sandy's back in the office?"

My pulse revved its engine, but I tried to ignore it. "Uh, no. I can meet you." Blessedly, Haven had looked back down at her computer screen. "Do you prefer a house or apartment?"

My fluster level was an eleven on a scale that topped out at ten. It was a freaking call with a guy about a rental. OMG.

I mustered every ounce of composure and willed my pulse to slow its galloping beat and the heat rising inside to dissipate.

"I'm under contract to buy a house, but in the short term, I need a rental. It doesn't really matter as long as it's a month-to-month lease."

"Um, okay, that makes sense." For fuck's sake, how many times was I going to start a sentence with um?

"Um, we're pretty flexible. We have some small houses available month to month right downtown."

"Can I see one?"

"Of course," I practically chirped. I took a slow breath.

"Tell me when and where."

I gazed at the clock on the wall above my office door. "How about in half an hour? It's right off Main Street. Just go past Spill the Beans Café and take the next left toward the harbor. You will see four houses in a row that look the same on the outside. Park in front of them, and I'll meet you there."

"Looking forward to seeing you in a half hour," Jack said, his voice all gruff and rumbly.

My hormones were convinced he was looking forward to seeing me for more than just a rental and went a little wild. My body felt like the inside of a pinball machine.

As soon as I hung up, Haven's eyes whipped up from her laptop. "Wow. I think you might like Jack Hamilton."

"Haven," I warned.

"What? You deserve to like someone. It's fun."

I let out a small sigh. "I don't date."

"I've noticed," she said pointedly. "What's that all about?"

"Seriously? Anyone interested in me in this town wants a connection with my family. I don't have many other reasons, but that's enough."

Haven studied me briefly before she shrugged lightly and graciously let me off the hook. "I understand. Don't get me wrong, I love Rhys. But there's so much pressure in the world to find love. Maybe you have the hots for Jack Hamilton, and he sure *is* cute."

She waggled her brows. "But no pressure from me on dating."

"You try dating with older brothers," I offered wryly. That was another easy excuse.

There was more to this, but I didn't want to discuss it. My brothers assumed I was cynical, but they didn't even know the whole story. It was deeply personal. Even though we were tight as siblings and we all collectively adored our mother and missed our father, our father's early death had led to a series of events that created lots of pain and damage in the family.

"Where are we with these plans?" I asked Haven, eager to change the subject. "Let's settle on this before I leave."

Haven shifted around the edge of the conference table, sliding her laptop closer to me.

"What do you think?" Haven was a graphic designer and an artist. She did handmade invitations and the like, but she also handled all the graphics for our corporate events. It was such a relief to have someone truly creative who I trusted.

I studied what she had on her screen. The cheerful and whimsical graphic had, of course, our telltale fire-weed woven along the edges of the design.

"It's perfect." I beamed at her.

"I'll polish it up and send the final version to you before tomorrow." She paused, a sly gleam entering her gaze. "Now, go crush on Jack Hamilton for a little while."

I rolled my eyes as I stood up. "I can enjoy the view."

Chapter Seven

MCKENNA

I zipped up my coat as I walked down the sidewalk, careful to step around the few icy patches. February in Fireweed Harbor was usually the coldest time of winter. In another month, the cold weather would ease up. We couldn't count on spring until April or May, but we got glimpses of warmer days. I loved the contrast of winter and enjoyed how pretty the landscape was.

I breathed in the crisp, icy air. My pulse picked up when I turned onto the street where Jack was meeting me, and I mentally insisted it was only because of my brisk pace.

A black truck was parked ahead, and I watched as Jack stepped out. I managed a shallow breath and ignored my racing pulse. He rounded his truck and waited on the sidewalk for me. My hormones stood and clapped, letting out a raucous cheer at the sight of Jack with his dark hair and impossibly blue eyes. Stopping before him, my gaze traced along his angled cheekbones and strong, square jaw.

He dipped his chin. "Good afternoon." His lips kicked up at one corner.

My belly spun, executing a happy little flip. "Hi," I squeaked.

"Thanks for taking the time to show me the house. I feel like I'm asking you to do extra."

"Not at all," I insisted. "I usually cover for Sandy when she's out."

"The houses all look the same, like you said," Jack said as he turned to face them.

Our property management company owned properties all over Fireweed Harbor and other areas in Alaska. These homes were mini Cape-style homes. They each had one dormer upstairs and two windows downstairs, flanking a central door and cute front porches.

Our property management business was a small part of the corporation. Fireweed Industries was initially just a winery, a little passion project of our grandmother's. That had expanded into a brewery, a restaurant, and more. Once money began to flow, our earlier generation invested wisely, taking advantage of the oil boom in Alaska. Those investments had been the springboard for the business to become a multinational corporation, one of the largest hailed from Alaska. We had our headquarters in Seattle for years, but when my eldest brother Rhys took over fully as CEO, he decided to bring us back home to Fireweed Harbor. With the internet, we didn't need to be in a major city anymore to run the business.

We were all glad to be back in Fireweed Harbor. Recently, we'd invested heavily in shifting from fossil fuel projects to renewable energy resources. Our long-term plan was already beginning to pay off, thanks to the vision of Rhys and our cousin Archer.

I ran public relations for the entire corporation. I loved my job.

"Do I get my pick?" Jack quipped as his gaze scanned the houses.

I pointed at the one on the very end. "That's the only one available." It happened to be where Rhys and Haven lived for a while before they finished building their new home. With a toddler, they definitely needed more space than these small houses offered.

Jack glanced down, his eyes crinkling with his smile. Tingles radiated outward through me.

"Follow me." We walked up the steps, and I punched in the code on the keypad.

Jack held the door for me, and I told myself I didn't need to swoon over him being polite. We stepped inside, and I ordered my hormones to chill out. They weren't listening, but I tried. I swung an arm around the space. "Here it is."

I gestured around the living room area downstairs with light-colored hardwood flooring and tall windows. "There's even a fireplace." Jack's low laughter sent a sizzle of heat zipping up my spine. "There's the kitchen. No table but a counter with stools. That staircase takes you to a small loft area. There's a single bedroom with a nice en suite bathroom upstairs." He nodded along as my words tumbled out in a nervous rush. "There's a half bath and laundry through there." I paused to take a breath. I was just ridiculous, getting all worked up over showing a rental. "Go ahead and walk around."

He strolled around the downstairs while I refused to look at him. My hormones were going insane. They were raising a ruckus and making me hot all over.

I rested my hips against the counter and checked my email on my phone. I needed something to distract me. A few minutes later, I heard Jack come downstairs. He walked into the downstairs bathroom. I was point- lessly trying to read a spreadsheet on my phone and didn't hear him come out.

I jumped when he said, "I'm in."

My hand flew to my chest, an unwelcome sense of fear racing through me. I turned quickly.

Jack's brows arched up. "Definitely didn't mean to startle you."

I nodded, my heart pounding in an unsteady beat as my brain tried to convince my body there was nothing to freak out about. "Uh, what do you think?"

"I think I'll take it," he said dryly. "That was a fore- gone conclusion, honestly. I need a place, and this is perfect."

"Are you sure? Do you need to know the rent or anything?"

"You're not gonna rip me off, are you?" he teased.

My cheeks felt hot as I shook my head.

"I just have one request."

"What's that?"

"Can I see the back porch?"

Chapter Eight

JACK

McKenna's gray eyes blinked up at me. "The porch?" Before I could even reply, she shook her head as if to herself. "Of course."

She slipped past me, her arm brushing mine. That glancing touch sent a little jolt of electricity radiating outward. McKenna had an unsettling effect on me, and I wasn't sure what to make of it.

Of course, she was beautiful. I still recalled the first time I'd seen her. Stepping out of my room on the ferry, I'd unintentionally opened the door right into her face. Even in the jumble of that moment, she'd been stunning. Just as she was now.

"There!" She swung the door open, and the crisp winter air gusted inside in a little swirl.

Reflexively, I reached above her, opening the door wider and gesturing her through. "Go ahead."

After a beat of hesitation, she sidled past me. She carried a sweet scent, barely there with a hint of vanilla. I wanted to step closer and breathe her in. I followed her out onto the back deck. Just like the rest of the house, it was cute.

The small covered porch offered a view of the mountains and the harbor. There were two matching chairs and snow-covered flower boxes.

McKenna wrapped her arms around her waist, looking out toward the harbor. I wanted to step closer and slide my arms around her. My reaction to her was unexpected. Rather than dissipating, it was like an engine revving louder and faster.

"It sure is pretty here," I offered.

Her eyes slid to mine. Her cheeks were a little pink from the cold. "It is."

"Do you ever get tired of the view?"

She shook her head quickly. "Never."

"Have you always lived here?"

"I was born and grew up here, but then I went away for college. Until about two years ago, we had our headquarters in Seattle."

Our conversation was mundane, with nothing remarkable about it at all. Yet the entire time I looked at her, it felt as if sparks shimmered in the air. Chemistry sparked like a live wire between us.

In spite of that, I could also feel her reaction to it. She might as well have been waving a stop sign. I understood that all too well. She shivered, tightening her arms around her waist. That galvanized me.

"Let's go back inside." I reached for the doorknob, and it didn't move. "It's locked."

McKenna let out a huff. "It has an automatic lock. I always forget." She reached into her pocket before rolling her eyes. "I left the keys inside in my purse. The front door has a keypad. I'll go around front."

I glanced at the snow piled up around the edges of the porch. Just as I was about to offer to go around front myself, McKenna jumped off the steps into the snow.

I immediately followed. She glanced over her shoulder. "Are you worried about me in the snow? I can handle some snow. I grew up here." She threw one arm in an arc. "I love snow! I can totally deal with it."

"Okay, Miss I-can-totally-deal-with-it, I can too. But I can't wait on the porch while you walk through the snow by yourself."

With another glance back, she rolled her eyes. "It's barely above my knees." Her voice drifted over her shoulder as she turned forward again.

I chuckled. "Barely above your knees," I muttered as I eyed the snow that was easily halfway up her thighs.

Her throaty laughter sizzled like a bolt of lightning in my system. Fuck me. This woman had tapped deep into a vein of need.

When she rounded the front corner of the house, her footsteps faltered, and she stumbled, letting out what sounded like a painful yelp.

I clambered through the snow to her side. "Are you okay?" I reflexively reached to steady her.

She drew in a breath through her teeth. "There's a stupid boulder here. It's decorative." She looked up at me. "I forgot it was here."

I glanced down to see that her jeans were torn where she scraped her knee, enough that a little blood was in the snow.

I wasn't even thinking when I stepped closer and lifted her into my arms.

"What are you doing?" Her eyes were wide when I glanced down.

"You're bleeding." As if that explained everything.

"I can walk," she insisted.

"Your jeans are torn, your knee is bleeding, and we're almost to the front of the house."

"Well, don't you—" She began just when my knee collided with the very boulder in question that had already left its mark on her.

"Fuck!" I stepped around it, ignoring the sharp pain.

I started to take another step when McKenna began with, "There's another —"

My other leg ran into a hard rock, and we fell together. I cushioned her fall by rolling quickly. Seconds later, she sat on my lap in the snow. Her surprise shifted from giggling to full-on belly laughs.

McKenna's laugh was infectious. Moments later, we stared at each other as we tried to catch our breaths. Her laughter petered out, punctuated by a hiccup.

"Wow," she finally said. "That's what you get for trying to be chivalrous."

"I'd do it all over." I was completely serious. McKenna laughing in my arms as we sat after falling in the snow felt incredibly good.

We were both dusted with snow. I finally noticed the cold underneath me. McKenna was warm in contrast. My body revved its engine at the feel of her soft curves. She looked at me again. Her cheeks were flushed pink, her lips parted, and her tongue darted out to swipe across her bottom lip.

The urge to kiss her was fierce. As we stared at each other, I had no idea how much time passed. For that moment, it was just McKenna and me on a crisp, snowy day, tangled up in the snow. Her gaze sobered, and her lashes swept down.

"I want to kiss you, McKenna." My voice was a gruff whisper.

The soft curves of her breasts pressed against me with the motion of her breath. Her eyes closed again.

I didn't know much about her, just a sketch of the outlines of her life, but I sensed a deep cynicism, almost as if a door was closed in a shadowy space. When she opened her eyes again, all the lingering laughter had disappeared.

"It's nothing more than a kiss. It's not worth it," she said.

Before I could say anything, she scrambled off my lap. Seconds later, she was on her feet, holding her hand out to me. I took it and stood. I let my gaze travel over her. I could see that bloody scrape on her knee. "Let's get you cleaned up."

"You don't have to help. I can take care of myself."

Ah, so that was how it was going to be.

I wanted to say more, to press. But instead, I watched as she turned. When I belatedly began, "McKenna, let me —"

She glanced over her shoulder. "Really. You don't need to save everyone, Jack. I just scraped my knee."

Chapter Nine

MCKENNA

My breath came out in a startled gasp. "Ow, ow, ow, ow!" I exclaimed to myself.

I dabbed antiseptic cleaner over the scrape on my knee. I was alone in the bathroom in the house three doors down from Jack. I was between places, still trying to decide where I wanted to live.

I let out a little sigh. I kind of hoped he never noticed I lived just a few doors away from him. I'd had my own place in Seattle, but I'd yet to find a permanent place back here in Fireweed Harbor. Seeing as I'd been one of the squeaky wheels about wanting to be back in Alaska, I couldn't complain.

Somehow, coming home felt like opening the doors for too many closets. I thought I'd effectively locked all the hatches in my heart. Instead, skeletons that had been tucked away were rattling their way out.

There was a sharp knock on my door, and I nearly jumped out of my skin and banged my head on the shelf on the wall behind me in the process. Speaking of skeletons, I had the worst startle reflex, and I hated it.

I took a slow breath. Letting it out, I grabbed the large bandage I'd set on the counter before I began cleaning the scrape and quickly smeared antibiotic cream on my knee before slapping the bandage over it. I yanked on a pair of leggings and hurried out of my bathroom.

I could see Tessa's silhouette through the window. She held up a bottle of wine and waved. My rampaging pulse began to slow. "Come in!"

Tessa called through the window, "The door is locked."

"Oh right." I always locked my door. Fireweed Harbor was safe, but old habits die hard and all that. I swung it open with a smile. "You're here first."

"I'm right here!" Haven's voice carried up the walkway behind Tessa. I chuckled, widening the door as she approached.

"Come on in. Do we know if Rosie can make it?"

Tessa was already crossing the living room and heading for the island in the kitchen that divided the two spaces. "She's finishing up at the hospital, and then she's coming over. She wants pizza," Tessa said over her shoulder.

"I already ordered it on the way over," Haven chimed in.

I closed the door behind Haven. "Perfect."

Haven lifted her large purse over her shoulder and fished out two bottles of mead from my family's brewery. "Samples, so they were free." She waggled her brows.

"You don't have to pay." I rolled my eyes.

"That just feels weird to me." She dropped her purse on the floor by the island and slipped onto a stool, sliding both bottles onto the counter and tapping them lightly with her fingertips.

"If you ever have a baby, it's so great when you're done nursing, and you can just have something to drink and not stress about it," she added.

"You mean you don't want to do the whole pumping and flushing of your breast milk? It's so much fun," Tessa said dryly.

Haven shook her head slowly. "That seemed like too much trouble. Honestly, I had so much trouble with nursing that I didn't nurse for long. I'm aware of those people who insist that nursing until your baby is walking and talking is important, but it wasn't for me. Jake had trouble latching on, and it was a constant struggle. He did so much better with a bottle. I pumped for six months. My doctor told me to stop feeling guilty because I had trouble producing enough milk, but I still feel guilty about it."

I glanced at my friends as I sat down across from Haven. "There is so much guilt that comes with being a mother. I don't want to have kids."

"The guilt is real," Haven said. "Like tonight, Rhys is home with little Jake, and I feel like I'm supposed to be there."

I eyed her. "Don't. You're home most nights. Rhys is my brother, and I love him very much, but even the guys who try don't carry as much as the moms."

"Definitely not," Tessa said. "I'm kicking ass at the single mom thing, though."

"You know, you don't talk much about him, but what is the scoop on your ex? All I know is the divorce was ugly," Haven commented. "I was living out of town when you two were together."

Tessa turned from the kitchen cabinets where she was fetching some glasses and set them on the counter. "I married an asshole. He's still doing his damnedest to make my life a living hell. Rich does not give two shits about our son, but he sure cares about making my life difficult with custody demands in court."

"But what happened?" Haven pressed.

Tessa sat down, and we all poured our drinks. I chose the blackberry honey mead.

"Rich was very charming. Until he wasn't. If I were to tell you some of the things he said to me, I don't know if you'd believe me. It's too embarrassing to even talk about. My therapist says he's emotionally abusive and used emotional manipulation to control me. I'm so ashamed of it. Even with that, I have Eric and wouldn't trade him for the world. I'd go through all that hell again if I had to." Tessa's eyes were bright with tears, but she lifted her chin high. "I'm grateful I finally found the strength to leave."

Haven and I were quiet before Haven offered, "I'm so sorry."

I leaned close to Tessa and curled my arm around her shoulders to give her a fierce squeeze.

When I leaned back, she glanced back and forth between us. "Thank you. I'm lucky to have friends like you all. And even though I'm stuck dealing with Rich because of our son, I can deal with it now. I'm okay." She took a swallow of her drink. "Now, let's talk about you." Tessa's gaze swung to me.

"What about me?" I hedged.

"Well, I hear Jack Hamilton will be moving in three houses down." Haven's eyes twinkled as she smiled at me. "And he sure is easy on the eyes."

"Sure is," Tessa teased. "Plus, he's got the whole firefighter thing going on. He's not just easy on the eyes, he saves people and forests."

I couldn't help but giggle. "Good point."

"Well?" Haven pressed, circling her hand in the air.

I willed my cheeks not to heat. "Well, what?"

"I know you think he's cute. And we all noticed how he looked at you at the wedding," she pointed out.

"That was months ago." I tried playing it cool, but I couldn't help my next question. "What do you mean by how he looked at me at the wedding?"

Tessa threw her head back with her laugh. "He was checking you out."

Just then, a knock on the door startled me enough that I jumped again.

"It's just Rosie," Haven said.

Rosie was already opening the door as I called out, "Come in!"

Rosie shook some snow off her jacket as she closed the door behind her. "It started snowing." She hung her jacket on the coat rack beside my door and slipped out of her boots.

"How much?" Tessa asked.

Rosie crossed the room, sitting down beside me. "Not too much. When I was leaving the hospital, I checked the weather, and it said light snow this evening. But it looks like we have a snowstorm coming in this weekend. I just hope it's not too bad. I don't mind the snow personally, but it always means a busy weekend at the hospital. I'm covering two shifts because one of the other nurses is out of town."

Haven slid an empty glass in front of Rosie just as there was another knock on the door. This time, it was the pizza delivery guy. As I walked toward the door, Haven called out, "I already paid for it. Just make sure to give him a good tip."

I did as instructed, thanking the guy and saying, "Drive safe," as he jogged down the stairs. The flurries glittered in the streetlights.

A few minutes later, we were all eating. "Back to the point, so Jack was checking you out at the wedding." Tessa waggled her brows before she took a bite of her pizza slice.

Rosie slid her eyes to me. She grinned but didn't offer anything.

"Why are you looking at me?" I couldn't hide the defensiveness in my voice.

"Jack was also checking you out at the café the other morning," Rosie replied.

"You weren't even there," I protested.

"I came in after you left, and Hazel told me all about it." Rosie's grin was sly.

I chuckled softly as I shook my head. "Oh, I love living in a small town when I don't hate living in a small town."

"You and Jack would make gorgeous children," Haven pointed out.

"Well, that's beside the point, seeing as I have no interest in having kids."

"None?" Tessa pressed.

"None," I said flatly.

I wasn't certain about many things in life, but this was one of them. I'd never had that whole got-to-have-a-baby feeling. My own childhood had soured me on children. Aside from my family's tangled, messy history, I had my own secrets to keep. I feared that having a child would make things way too messy. In a way, I was relieved I didn't crave it. I didn't want to worry about it.

Rosie nodded firmly. "I think it's good you know that."

Haven looked back and forth between us. "Really?"

"Really. All of you know my family's history. I love my brothers, and I love my mom, but we all went through a lot as kids. I'm good on my own. I've never craved to have a family or a baby, so that makes it easy."

Rosie chimed in, "Not everybody needs to have kids. Trust me, at the hospital, I see a parade of people coming through who probably shouldn't have had kids. I don't mean it to be judgy. The *idea* of kids is totally different from the reality. Speaking of your family, your mom is awesome. As far as I know, your dad was too, but he died when you were all pretty young. And then along came your grandfather to help." She shook her head slightly and let out a sigh.

"If you consider verbally abusing all of us, being a brutal asshole, and knocking around some of my brothers as *helping*," I said sarcastically. They all knew my family's story or most of it.

My pulse raced from just speaking about my grandfather. His shadow over our family was long and dark.

Tessa's understanding gaze met mine. "I'm sorry."

I shrugged. "It's okay. It's in the past. You still have to deal with your ex."

"I wouldn't change a thing when it comes to my son, but—" She paused, taking a sip of her drink. "Children are complicated. Eric's a gift in my life, but I worry about how I can protect him from his father. Even though I feel so blessed to have Eric, I'm concerned he'll feel differently when he's older."

We all sat quietly for a minute. Because that was the catch. Tessa was an amazing mom and a fierce protector of her son. But she could never change who his father was and how he treated them.

Rosie cocked her head to the side as she studied Tessa. "It'll be okay. There is no perfect, not for any life, not for any child. Eric's got you, and that's a lot."

Tessa smiled over at her, straightening her shoulders. "And three of the best unofficial aunts in the universe."

We toasted to that, and talk shifted to lighter matters. Later that night, after my friends left, I considered the conversation. I'd always known I didn't want kids. It was a decision I didn't doubt. There was that, and then the idea of being serious in any relationship. *That* made me skittish. There was always the pull to wonder. You just never knew what someone could turn into and what could happen.

My parents had wanted a big family and had one. Then our father died when I was only a toddler. I had no memory of him.

While I wished I could maybe find a good partner in life, I knew what loss felt like. Even though I hadn't known my father, he was still this empty hole in my life, a gap of nothing other than wishes and hopes. If I had a father. If, if, if...

I shook those thoughts away, and my mind spun to Jack and my friends' teasing about him. Sure, he *was* hot, and we definitely had chemistry. The whole casual thing had never really worked out for me, but I wondered with Jack. Maybe he would be worth the risk.

Chapter Ten

JACK

The automated voicemail message droned in my ear. As soon as it beeped for me to leave a message, I said, "Hey, it's your brother. Again. Please call me. Love you, asshole."

I tapped the screen to end the call and leaned my head back as I took a slow breath. A year ago, my brother got some shitty fucking news. After three rounds of chemo, his lung cancer was back. The odds weren't good, and he didn't want more treatment. To make it even shittier, he didn't smoke, never had. The best guess was exposure to radon gas from living in an area where it was common in homes. Fun facts: radon gas was the largest source of radiation exposure for people who lived in Washington state, and radon exposure was the second leading cause of lung cancer.

His life, for now, was a ticking time bomb. One I would just have to live with.

"Fuck," I said to the sky.

"What the hell did the sky do to you?" A voice came from in front of me. I leveled my gaze and found a man standing a few feet away.

I shrugged. "Sometimes life is just shit. In this case, it's not my bad luck, but it still pisses me off."

The guy cracked a dry smile, but the look in his eyes was serious. Maybe he didn't know my story, yet I sensed he knew a little bit about bad luck.

"Well, not gonna argue that point." His boots crunched on the frozen gravel as he closed the distance between us, holding his hand out.

I shook it, and his grip was firm and dry. He wasn't one to linger on a handshake either, which I appreciated. "I'm Hudson Fox, the superintendent for the hotshot crew here. You look a lot like Jack Hamilton."

I chuckled. "I am Jack Hamilton. We met over video, but the reception was a little spotty, and you were sitting at a table in the back."

"I fucking hate video conferences," he grumbled.

"Understood. Can't say I love them. They are convenient, though."

"True that. Welcome. We're glad to have you." He dipped his head. "Want to come inside, or would you like to curse at the sky some more?"

A laugh rustled in my throat. "The sky can't help, and it's definitely not the sky's fault. Let's go inside. Let me grab my bag."

I took a few steps back toward my truck to grab the gear bag out of the passenger seat that had traveled with me for the past few years. I kicked the door shut with my foot as I slung the bag over my shoulder.

Hudson already held open the door to the back of the building. He gestured me in with a flourish. Hudson had rumpled brown curls, bright green eyes, and an easygoing smile.

It was midmorning, a few minutes before he'd texted me to come in today. For, as he put it, "the official tour."

"Right this way." He walked past me, and I followed. "I don't think there's much different here than other stations you've been in." He thumbed to his left. "Break room and laundry in there." He gestured in the other direction. "Showers there." The hallway opened up, and he paused by a row of lockers, rapping his knuckles on a locker to one side. "You can toss your bag in there. We share the space with the town crew."

"Good to know," I said, quickly chucking my bag into an empty locker.

"Come on in here. I'm not sure who will be around today. Winter is pretty quiet. We help on town calls here and there, do training, and so on. We might be out for a few stretches if we get called to the Lower 48. For the most part, though, you can consider roughly November to March the best time to take a vacation if you want one. You mentioned you were buying a house." At my nod, he continued. "I'd get settled now. Summer is nuts. We have a few quiet stretches, but that's about it. Follow me."

I followed him down the rest of the short hallway, which opened into a large room. A kitchen area had several round tables and chairs nearby. Two large sectional couches sat in front of a TV mounted on the wall. Beyond that was a glass-enclosed workout room. All of this was fairly standard for fire stations.

A few guys were working out, and some lounged on the couch. "Hey!" Hudson called out to the room at large. "Jack's here."

The two guys seated on the couch glanced over. "Hey, hey," one of them said as he stood from the couch, approaching to shake my hand as we walked over.

"Leo, Jack. Jack, Leo," Hudson said as he pointed back and forth.

Leo grinned. "Nice to meet you in person."

The other guy turned off the TV and stood. He held his hand out to shake mine. "Kincaid," he said simply.

"Jack. Good to meet you."

"These guys are on the hotshot crew," Hudson explained. "We used to work together up in Fairbanks."

"You should come with us tonight to locals' night at the winery," Leo said.

"I've heard about that."

"Food's good, drinks are good, and it's always a good place to hang out. Hope you don't mind being in a small town," Kincaid chimed in.

"Not at all. I grew up outside of Seattle in a small town in the foothills of the Cascades. This is my first full winter in Alaska. I have family in Diamond Creek, so I spent the first half of this winter with them."

"Nice," Leo replied. "So you're technically local."

I chuckled. "I don't know about that. Alaska is pretty big."

"It's big geographically but small otherwise," Hudson said.

"Nice ski lodge in Diamond Creek," Kincaid added.

"That ski lodge happens to be owned by my cousins."

Kincaid let out a little whistle. "Sweet. Pretty place."

"It sure is. It was impossible for me to get out of shape while I was there. I helped out as one of the first responders for their emergency team. They've got hundreds of miles of cross-country ski trails in addition to the downhill ones. I stayed busy. Nice work, though. View's always a stunner every way you look."

A few other guys wandered in before Hudson took me on a full tour. After that, I worked out. I needed it.

Just as I climbed into my truck to leave a while later, my cell rang. I glanced at the screen and answered immediately. "Hey."

"Hey," Derek replied.

"You know, people get worried when you don't call back."

My heart burned a little at the sound of his voice. It was strained. I knew my brother was tired. My plan was to bring him up here to stay with me. I had already confirmed we could get the medical monitoring he needed. After his last miserable bout with chemo, he decided to just face his odds.

"I know," he said, his voice thready. "I was just getting all my ducks in a row. I think I can be up there in about two months. I might be pretty sick by then. Are you sure you want me to do this?"

"Yes."

I'd honestly never been more certain of anything in my life. My brother was my best friend, and it was going to hurt like fucking hell, but I was determined to be there for him. If he wanted to spend the last months of his life in Alaska with me, then that was what we would do.

"If you change your mind and want to do treatment, I'm there. We'll figure it out one way or another," I added.

I hadn't told my brother that I'd gone behind his back to confirm we could get him the help he needed in Juneau if he changed his mind. "I close on the house next month."

"I'll be there. All right. Love you, man," he said,

clicking to end the call before I could return the sentiment.

I blinked away the tears stinging my eyes and took a steadying breath before I turned my truck on. Moments later, I was driving down to my temporary house when I saw McKenna walking down the sidewalk with grocery bags dangling from her arms. She turned to climb the steps of a house only three doors from mine.

As I watched, she slipped on the ice, and groceries spilled everywhere. I heard a muffled, "Fuck!"

I slowed to pull over and park, climbing out quickly and jogging over to her. "Are you okay?"

Chapter Eleven

MCKENNA

"Shit," I muttered under my breath.

I was sprawled on the icy walkway with groceries strewn around me. And, of course, Jack Hamilton just had to be the one to drive up. Now, he was trying to be helpful. My knee throbbed.

As luck would have it, I'd managed to slide and jam my knee against the edge of the stairs. "I'm fine. I can deal with it," I said as he stopped beside me.

Jack's gaze arced about the groceries surrounding me. "Are you sure about that?" he asked, his tone dry as sand.

I let out a sigh, ignoring my achy knee. I shifted and started to stand only to lose my footing again. "Stupid ice."

Jack was already reaching out to steady me. "Ice is definitely a stupid asshole." His tone was somber as he looked down at me, but his eyes twinkled.

A giggle slipped out. "Okay, fine. Maybe I don't have this."

"Let me help."

He gathered up my groceries in no time. I fished in

the snow along the edge of the walkway to rescue some cans that had rolled free. A few moments later, we walked into my small house.

Jack glanced around. "Does another tenant get grocery duty?"

I looked up at him, pondering my options, and decided to go with honesty. "I live here."

"Oh, you're my neighbor?"

I shrugged, not sure why I hadn't said as much when I showed him the rental the other day.

"Fireweed Harbor is really small. Everyone's your neighbor."

Jack studied me for a minute before walking past me to set the bags of groceries on the kitchen island. He turned back. "I suppose so, but not everyone lives three houses down."

"Good point." I shrugged again and began putting away the groceries.

Just having him around made me restless in my skin. Nervous energy buzzed through me a little faster than usual.

"Thank you for your help," I belatedly said as I turned back to face him.

"Of course. I imagine you'd help me if I slipped on the ice."

"Definitely. I'd help a stranger if they slipped on the ice. I'm sure you would too."

Jack nodded slowly, his eyes holding mine. I shifted on my feet, trying to ignore how my pulse hummed faster and faster. My belly did a little shimmy.

I didn't know how long we stared at each other, but my body was alive with heat and electricity. I startled myself when I whispered, "Jack..."

Perhaps a foot separated us, maybe less. When I

slid my hand along the counter, my fingertips touched his.

He moved to push away from me, and I experienced an intense shaft of disappointment. In another second, he stood in front of me and curled his hands over the edge of the counter, catching me between his arms.

Jack's intense blue eyes held mine. "Tell me something, McKenna."

"What?" I rasped.

"Can I kiss you?"

I nodded before my mind could tell me that was a bad idea. I didn't kiss people. Kisses led to nothing but disappointment.

"Are you sure?" he prompted.

Perhaps my doubts flickered in my eyes. *What the hell? It's just a kiss.*

Maybe it would be a good kiss, a little memory to tuck in my pocket.

"Yes." My voice was low, barely there. "But why?" My doubts crowded their way forward, pushy and demanding.

"Because I want to kiss you," Jack said simply.

We stared at each other. The air around us felt as if a storm waited, burgeoning with a force about to unleash.

He took another step closer, and I could feel the heat of him, the power of him. He dipped his head slowly, his eyes on mine the entire time. My own eyes fell closed just as his lips brushed over mine. That subtle contact was like a lick of fire. My breath drew in sharply.

His lips were soft and warm. He lingered for a moment before drawing back to look at me. When I dragged my eyes open, whatever he saw in them caused him to step even closer.

His next kiss was slow and lingering. I let out a soft sigh, my mouth opening, and his tongue swept in. Our kiss went from testing the waters to deep diving into the depths. I distantly heard a soft whimper in the back of my throat. I shifted closer, arching into him, and slid one of my hands around his waist. My fingers pressed into the banded cords of his muscled back.

He angled his head to the side, claiming my mouth. I wanted *more*. He tasted a little minty and smelled like salt-scoured ocean air, fresh and clean, underlaid with an earthy, masculine scent.

By the time we broke apart, I was nearly desperate for air. I gulped in deep lungfuls. We stared at each other, eyes wide.

I was taken aback, almost shocked at the force of that kiss, at the startling intimacy I felt flourishing between us. I was almost afraid of it.

Jack closed his eyes and shook his head sharply before opening them again. He studied me like he didn't know what to make of me.

"I don't think we can do that again," I said.

"Why not?"

Chapter Twelve

JACK

"Because," McKenna answered.

I knew any kind of entanglement wasn't a good idea. Uncomplicated was all I could hope for.

For me, McKenna was anything but uncomplicated. I'd met her when I accidentally gave her a black eye. I'd wanted her every second since.

Every moment I spent in her presence only amped up the intense attraction I felt for her. But it was more than that. I wanted to know why she was so guarded. I wanted to know all of her secrets. I wanted to know *her*.

————

The following morning, I walked into Spill the Beans Café. One of the women who owned the place smiled at me warmly. "Good morning, Jack," she said.

"Hazel, right?" I prompted as I stopped in front of the counter.

"Good memory." She winked.

"Good morning to you."

"Your usual?" she prompted.

"Do I have a usual? Am I that obvious?" I teased.

Hazel laughed. "You've been in here four times, and every single time, you've gotten plain black coffee, strong. Which suits you. You're that kind of guy."

"I am?" I couldn't help but ask.

Hazel shrugged. "Tall, dark, handsome, firefighter." She held one finger after another up. "It suits you to get plain black coffee. Although it might be more fun if you tried something sweet."

I couldn't help but chuckle. "Fair enough. What do you recommend?"

Her eyes widened. "Oh, this is going to be fun." She turned around, scanning the chalkboard mounted on the wall behind the counter. "I think you should get chocolate, slightly sweet. Honestly"—she turned back to face me—"some drinks are just too sweet. I promise you this one is pretty subtle. It's got a hint of chocolate and a touch of sweetness."

"Let's do it."

"Anything to eat? You don't have a usual for that," she said as she grinned over at me while preparing my coffee.

"Depends on my mood. Sometimes I want sweet, sometimes I want salty or savory, I suppose." I scanned the display case of baked goods. "I think I'll go with a spinach feta popover this morning."

"Good choice. And they just came out of the oven," she said, lowering her voice as if imparting a secret. She pulled one out of the case and slid it in the toaster. "Needs to be a little warmer, though. What do you think of Fireweed Harbor?" She returned to prepping my coffee.

"I love it so far. To state the obvious, it's beautiful. Everyone seems pretty friendly."

"Good. I hope you stay."

Just then, the door opened behind me. I glanced over my shoulder, but not so fast that I didn't miss Hazel narrowing her eyes.

A couple walked in, and it took me a minute, but I recognized the guy as the one who spread rumors about McKenna and did the podcast story on her family. The couple stopped by a table with the guy taking a call on his phone.

I glanced back at Hazel. "I heard he's a jerk," I said, keeping my voice low.

She shrugged a little. A few minutes later, she handed me my coffee and food. The guy had finished whatever call he'd taken, and now the couple appeared to be bickering.

As I walked past, I overheard the guy say, "Well, what exactly do you bring to this?"

The woman huffed. "Plenty. It's not all about money."

I kept walking, pushing through the door and outside into the crisp air. The girlfriend's comment about money brought McKenna to mind. I knew her family had money. Hell, I knew who they were before I even moved here. But her whole family was down to earth. Money just wasn't what I thought of with them.

Yet I imagine plenty of people, like say the asshole back there, whose sole motivation for wanting to be connected to the family was their money.

"Hey there," a voice said.

I lifted my eyes from the sidewalk in front of me to see Blake approaching.

"Well, hey there," I said, lifting my coffee in greeting. "Seems like I see you the most out of your family."

He shrugged. "We seem to go for our coffee about

the same time," Blake offered dryly. He glanced beyond my shoulder. "How do you like your place?"

"I rented it from your family's property management company. I'm not about to tell you if I don't like it," I teased.

He grinned. "You could."

"Nah, it's great. And it's just what I need. As I mentioned, I'm under contract to buy a house. I close next month, so I needed a short-term rental."

"Oh, right. Where's your house?"

I thumbed over my shoulder. "About five minutes that way on Emerald Road. It's got a nice view, enough space, and it was a good price."

"Oh, I know that place. The family who built it ended up moving a few months after they finished it. I'm guessing there's some finishing work to do."

"You guessed right, but I don't mind that at all."

"Do you need that much space? It's a three-bedroom house."

I paused for a beat, considering whether to tell him why I needed the space, but then I figured I might as well. It wouldn't be a secret.

"My brother is coming up to stay with me. He, uh, has cancer. It's pretty aggressive. He's already done three rounds of chemo and doesn't want to do more. He wants to be in Alaska. This way, he's got the space he needs."

Blake studied me for a moment before reaching out and clapping his hand on my shoulder, squeezing firmly. "That totally sucks, and I'm sorry. I'm glad you're going to be there for him. That's what I would do for anyone in my family. If you need anything, just, uh..." He released my shoulder, his words petering off. "Well, just let me know."

"I appreciate it. I went to see Derek during his last

round of treatment, and he was just fucking miserable. The odds are not good. So..." I took a breath to steel myself and keep the pain at bay. "I just want to be there for him. He's always been there for me. You'll meet him. He's a pretty social guy. I'm sure he'll be down here at the café gossiping with Hazel and Phyllis on the regular, even if he feels like hell."

Blake's eyes crinkled at the corners, although his gaze quickly shifted to somber again. "You never know how things will turn out."

I could sense he didn't know how to shift off the depressing part of this conversation. "You never do. I'll close on my house next month, and he'll move up sometime after that. They say he's got maybe a year without treatment. He wants to be here, so that's the plan."

Blake nodded. "If you need any help moving in, just give a shout."

"Good to know. Thanks, man. I'm sure I'll see you soon."

He clasped me on the shoulder once more as we passed. Walking down the street another moment later, I saw McKenna looking down at the sidewalk in front of the headquarters for Fireweed Industries. She rested her hand on her hip. As I got closer, I noticed she was looking at a kitten inside a planter box covered in snow.

I picked up my pace, stopping beside her. "That's one tiny kitten."

Chapter Thirteen

MCKENNA

I lifted my gaze from the tiny, shivering white kitten to Jack's. "Yeah, he or she is. I'm going to have to take it with me."

I leaned down and scooped the kitten up. The poor thing had to be close to frozen. I held it up for a minute before glancing at Jack. "She's a girl."

Unzipping the top of my coat, I tucked the kitten inside. "You're spending the day with me at work, Snowy."

"You can just show up with a kitten to work?" Jack asked.

I looked over at Jack and shrugged. "One of the few advantages to being a family member with an ownership stake in the corporation is being able to randomly show up with a kitten. I've never done it before, but it will be fine. I try not to pull rank, but I think this is important."

Jack's eyes were so blue and stunning that they took my breath away. When he smiled, my belly felt fluttery and liquid. "I think pulling rank in this case is critical," he said somberly with a teasing glint in his gaze. "I expect an update on how Snowy is doing later today."

Oh, how I wished I didn't react so strongly to Jack! But all the man had to do was smile, and my hormones were like a pinball machine, spinning and pinging and whistling.

"I'll give you an update," I managed.

"By the way, how's your knee?"

"The scrape has pretty much healed, just a little bruising left."

He nodded and winked. For fuck's sake! Now he was winking? My hormones didn't even know what to do with that.

"See you later." He lifted his coffee cup in a little wave and began walking.

Before I could think better of it, I called out, "Have you been to locals' night?"

He turned back. "I haven't, but the guys at the fire station tell me I should go."

"You should go. It's tonight."

He smiled again. "I might see you there."

My belly spun into several dizzying flips. I watched him walk off, my eyes lingering on his broad shoulders and his easy gait.

I peered down at the kitten tucked into my jacket. "What was I thinking?" I whispered to her.

She purred in response and nestled closer. She was still shivering, but it wasn't as bad.

———

"Hey, little!" Wyatt swept me into a bear hug. A moment later, he released me, and I turned, flinging my arms around his twin, Griffin.

Griffin chuckled as he gave me a back-slapping hug.

For my entire life, there was a joke with Griffin and Wyatt. Wyatt had always called me "little" as the youngest sibling in the family. Griffin countered that by treating me rough and tumble.

I stepped back, smiling at them a moment later. "I didn't know you two were coming into town."

Griffin and Wyatt were hotshot firefighters working on a crew up in Fairbanks. Of the two, Griffin seemed like he wanted to keep doing that for a little while longer. With Wyatt, I sensed he mostly wanted a reason not to be in Fireweed Harbor. On occasion, our messy group of siblings pondered why. I still didn't know the exact reason, but I knew Wyatt was the only sibling other than me who didn't revere Jake. Wyatt and I usually exchanged tight smiles whenever Jake came up.

Blake appeared at my shoulder, overhearing my comment. "Wyatt finally deigned to talk with me about taking over at the brewery." He glanced at Wyatt. "Dude, it's only another few months before I'll be desperate for you. I'm hoping you're not gonna make me beg."

Wyatt chuckled as Blake tugged him into a back-slapping hug and exchanged another with Griffin immediately after. Another moment later, Rhys and Haven arrived, expanding our circle. More hugs were given after Adam and Kenan appeared. We were stairsteps in age, with Rhys the oldest, followed by Blake, then two sets of twins, Kenan and Adam, Griffin and Wyatt, and then me. Our oldest brother Jake had died from alcohol poisoning in college.

His absence was a strange place in our family. Our mother grieved him terribly. My own feelings were, well, complicated. I didn't want to dwell on those feelings. I never did.

It was locals' night at Fireweed Winery. This was our flagship location. The winery and brewery had started it all. It was originally just a winery with my grandmother's homemade wines made from local berries, a very Alaskan way to start a business. From the land. So much of Alaska still felt close to the earth with the harsh, dark winters and short, bright summers.

It started as a lark because people loved her wines. It expanded into so much more. We still had the winery and restaurant, this one small piece of where it all began. Rhys had taken over as CEO of the international corporation. Our grandfather, abusive asshole that he was, had wisely invested in buying up land, energy projects, and more in Alaska. He folded that money into more and more.

Rhys had brought the company back home. Our cousin Archer was coordinating with Rhys to gradually transition a number of our holdings to renewable energy projects. It felt good to be back in Alaska. It was home for all of us.

Fiona appeared with her daughter, Lia. Fiona nudged me with her elbow before sliding her arm around my shoulders and giving me a squeeze. "Hey."

"Hey, hey," I returned. "You're not in the kitchen tonight?"

Fiona and Blake fell in love and got married after she took over the chef position for the winery. She shook her head. "Nope. I get to be a customer tonight."

A server passed by with a tray of drinks. He paused, and she greeted him before selecting a bottle of mead. Her daughter tugged to release her hand. "Mom, I want to say hi to Wyatt and Griffin."

Fiona leaned down, smoothing her daughter's hair

and tucking it behind her ears. "Okay. Stay close by all of us, though. Please."

Lia scampered off, and I glanced over at Fiona. "I'm glad you married Blake."

Fiona smiled. "I am too. But why do you say that now?"

I nudged my chin in the direction of Blake. "Because. He's happier since you've been together."

Although Lia was headed toward Wyatt and Griffin, she stopped beside Blake, and he lifted her in his arms to give her a big hug before setting her down. She chattered about something. His eyes were on her, all of his attention focused and warm.

Fiona's gaze sobered as she looked at them. "I think we all are. I feel lucky."

"You're both lucky."

Her smile was soft. "I'll agree. Meanwhile, how are things with you?"

I shrugged. "The same. Busy with work and life."

"What's this I hear about Jack?" she teased lightly.

I rolled my eyes, striving for a casual attitude. "Nothing. He's the latest handsome guy in Fireweed Harbor. And he's a hotshot firefighter."

Fiona held my gaze. "Do you even date?" she finally asked.

"Nope. I don't want kids, and I don't want marriage. I don't think I'm cut out for it."

"Oh?"

Her brows rose. "I have many questions on this topic." She paused, pursing her lips. "Actually, I don't. I never expected to meet Blake. But you know what I hated before I did?"

"What?"

"So many people having opinions that I must want some kind of relationship. Don't get me wrong, I love

Blake, and I'm really happy we're together. But life isn't all about that."

"Thank you for getting it. Most people don't."

She curled her arm around my shoulders, giving me another quick squeeze. "Social expectations are exhausting."

Just then, Wyatt circled to my other side and greeted Fiona. "The appetizers are amazing tonight."

She smiled. "I didn't make them tonight because I've been off all day."

"It's your menu, though," he pointed out.

Her cheeks flushed pink. "It is, so thank you."

The conversation moved along with my typical messy family babbling about work and other things. Rhys and Haven shared updates with Wyatt and Griffin about our nephew Jake. He was the second nephew of the family and named after our oldest brother. Before he died, Jake fathered a son that none of us had ever known about until his mom showed up, trying to claim Rhys was the father.

We had circled the wagons to welcome Matthew into the family. He didn't live in Fireweed Harbor, much to our mother's disappointment. We stayed in touch, and his mom brought him up sometimes while our mother visited them every few months.

Wyatt said something to my side when the conversation turned to our older brother Jake after Rhys made a teasing comment that Jake's namesake shared Jake's friendly nature.

"What?" I glanced at Wyatt.

He shrugged. After a long pause, he faced me fully, his gaze sobering. "Sometimes it gets old."

Anxiety kicked up inside, and my stomach churned. "Jake being so perfect?" I kept my voice low.

"Yep. I know he used to hit you," Wyatt said.

Chapter Fourteen

MCKENNA

My mouth dropped open. "You do?"

He nodded slowly. "I felt bad. Still do. I wish I'd been older back then. I didn't know what to do. You must get tired of hearing about how perfect he was supposed to be."

"Wyatt," I whispered, stepping closer. "What do you know?"

"Just that. One day, I was walking down the hallway. Jake was babysitting us, or I guess you 'cause you were the youngest. He told you to shut up, and you talked back. He hit you so hard you fell against the wall. I still feel bad. I'm really sorry I didn't do anything to stop it."

My lips felt numb, and static hummed in my brain. "I had no idea you knew," I finally whispered.

His throat worked as he swallowed and glanced around at our siblings. He brought his gaze back to mine. I recognized the sadness and anger held there. "I'm sorry. Griffin never saw it, but I told him what I saw, so he knows. After Jake died, we talked about it."

"Thank you." My voice was ragged.

"For not protecting you?" Wyatt countered.

"Wyatt, it wasn't your job to protect me. Just thank you for knowing what happened. Everyone else talks about Jake like he never did anything wrong. I know he went through horrible things, but he was never perfect. Not even close." I swallowed as a rush of pain rose inside, wicking tears into my throat and stinging my eyes.

Wyatt slid his arm around my shoulders, squeezing firmly. I took several deep breaths, savoring his steady, calming presence. I was starting to understand something. Wyatt kept his distance a little bit, and I thought maybe now I knew part of why.

We couldn't say anything more because Kenan and Quinn approached, leading to another round of hugs for Wyatt and Griffin.

I felt unsettled, restless, and reckless inside. I never talked to anyone in my family about what happened with Jake. All of us had borne the brunt of our grandfather's verbal abuse, but Jake and Rhys had been the targets of his physical abuse. We later found out that our grandfather had raped Jake. The pieces of the puzzle about why Jake drank himself to death had made sense.

In the aftermath of his death and the collective grief in our family, I had carried my own pain silently. Jake had hit me more than once. I was the annoying little sister. Even though, as an adult, I could intellectually understand Jake was only doing what he had learned, it didn't mean it was okay.

I wanted to escape my feelings frantically. I barely held it together while everyone talked and laughed around me.

I felt Jack before I saw him. His presence was electric. A prickle of awareness raced down my spine, reverberating with little pings of electricity gathering force.

Glancing over my shoulder, I saw him talking with Blake and Fiona a few feet away. His gaze locked onto mine. It felt as if a flame flickered through the air between us. He said something else to Blake before he turned to approach me.

Seconds later, Jack stopped in front of me. "Hello."

One word, two syllables. The rumbly sound of his voice sent pinwheels of fire spinning through me. I actually had to clear my throat to speak. "Hi."

Before Jack opened his mouth to say something else, Rhys interjected, "Hey, Jack. Glad you made it."

The usual round of greetings with my siblings began. Because my thoughts were muddled whenever I was near Jack, I forgot that he knew Wyatt and Griffin. I offered pointlessly, "They're hotshot firefighters up in Fairbanks."

Griffin waggled his brows as he grinned over at me. "We met on the ferry."

"Oh, that's right. I can blame my forgetfulness on my black eye."

Kenan appeared at that moment with Quinn, catching my last comment. "And you wore it well." He nudged me with his shoulder as Quinn laughed softly.

"How is Fireweed Harbor treating you?" Wyatt asked Jack.

"Good, so far. Thanks to McKenna here, I'm staying in one of your short-term rentals."

Just then, one of the servers appeared with another tray of drinks. Jack asked for recommendations, and everyone had an opinion. My mother appeared, beyond happy that all of us were here. She was always like that. The conversation continued, so Jack and I didn't really get to speak beyond that first hello. It

tended to be like that with my family. We were a big,
messy group.

Unfortunately for me, Jack lingered with my family.
I was annoyed with myself because I couldn't get my
freaking hormones to stand down, and I was wildly
unsettled by my conversation with Wyatt. With my
mother there, though, things got even worse. She'd
just returned from a trip visiting our nephew
Matthew.

"I just can't believe how much he looks like Jake,"
she gushed to Rhys.

I wanted to point out that Rhys looked a whole lot
like Jake, but I bit my tongue. We had strong genes.
With the exception of Kenan and Wyatt, we shared
dark blond hair and gray-blue eyes, while Wyatt and
Kenan had dark hair and blue eyes. Matthew could
easily be mistaken for Rhys's son at a glance.

I hated how much my mom revered Jake. I
reminded myself hundreds of times that nobody was
all good or bad. Good people sometimes did bad
things, and bad people sometimes did good things.
Life was made of shades of gray, and people were
complicated.

I loved Jake too, but I'd been his target, and
nobody but my therapist in college and me had
known. Until I'd learned Wyatt also knew. I felt his
eyes on me a few times during the night. I wanted to
ask him just how much he knew. I wanted to ask him
if he felt like me, sad but relieved that Jake had died. I
was tangled up with guilt because I felt like I had done
something to deserve being Jake's target. Intellectually,
I knew the truth. Jake had been a victim as well. I
reminded myself that not *all* hurt people hurt people.
For that reason alone, I hated that catchphrase.

I was feeling frantic to escape the feelings stirred

up inside. The hole Jake had left in our family was big. His loss was a tangled mess for all of us.

I took an unsteady breath and let it out. We were all careful about alcohol because Jake had drunk himself to death. Whenever I wanted to lose myself, to escape my feelings, I slammed the door on that false escape.

"How is the kitten?" Jack's voice came from above my shoulder.

I looked up. "Oh, she's good. I dropped her off at my place before I came here and scheduled a vet appointment."

He smiled. "Good to hear."

I managed a nod and nervously slid my fingers along the hem of my shirt. I must've looked as discombobulated as I felt because he prompted, "Are you okay?"

"Uh, sure. Just distracted." That wasn't a complete lie.

He studied me for a beat, and my belly shimmied and danced.

My mind flashed to the feel of his lips on mine. My body recalled the sweet escape he offered. My pulse raced along, faster and faster.

I thought maybe I could give in for once. Jack set off a chain reaction inside—raw chemistry, need, lust, and pure escape.

It *could* be uncomplicated. We didn't even have any history. He knew my family, but the connection was fresh.

I looked away, wanting to forget everything.

Jack was perfect for forgetting. The chemistry between us was its own bonfire, and he wouldn't gossip. He didn't know enough people in Fireweed Harbor to gossip.

"I have to say, this beer is excellent," Jack said at my shoulder.

I didn't even know how much time had passed since his last comment.

"Of course it is. It's from Fireweed Winery." I scrounged up my manners and a light, teasing tone.

"I'm serious," he added.

"I know. When I lived in Seattle, I must've tried every competitor for beer, wine, and mead, and we definitely hold our own. You'll have to try some of the wines and meads."

"Do you all host a locals' night every Wednesday?"

"We do." I took a swallow from my bottle of mead. I'd barely managed three sips tonight. I was too unsettled with everyone talking about Jake. It's not that he didn't come up often. Frankly, he came up way too much. I kind of wished Wyatt and Griffin would move home so that whenever they were here, my mom wouldn't get caught up in her wistful thinking about having everyone together and missing Jake all over again.

"Do you come every week?" Jack prompted, his voice puncturing my messy train of thought.

"Most of the time."

"Most of the time?" Wyatt interjected. "If I'm taking over as the brewer, I expect you here every week," he teased.

"Then you'd better take that job."

"And what about you?" I caught Griffin's eyes.

"What about me?" he returned.

I arched a brow. "Rumor has it you're considering one of the firefighter positions here." I gestured to Jack. "You guys could be on a crew together unless you want to go completely crazy and work for the family."

Griffin chuckled. "I'm not opposed to working for

the family. I just enjoy firefighting right now. To answer your question, I met with the superintendent for the new hotshot crew today. I'm thinking of coming down here this summer. It'll be the start of the last few years of my life as a firefighter. Can't do it forever."

"I do wish you would take another job," my mother interjected. "I love you both, but it's a high-risk job. I've already lost one son."

Griffin handled this guilt trip easily. "We know that, Mom. We all lost Jake. And we love you. No matter what, it's looking like Wyatt and I will be in Fireweed Harbor this summer."

With the shift in conversation, I took that moment to slip away. I reminded myself I loved my family. I just wished some things were different.

I popped into the kitchen to check on things. I knew I should go out front and say my goodbyes, but I didn't feel like it. I went out the back, stepping into the crisp, cold night. For just a moment, the noise from the kitchen spilled out through the doorway before the sounds muffled when the door clicked shut.

My boots scuffed on the frozen gravel as I began walking.

Chapter Fifteen

JACK

I felt my phone vibrate in my pocket, but I ignored it. Until it vibrated again and yet again. Clearly, somebody wanted to talk to me.

When there was a break in the conversation at Fireweed Winery, I said my goodbyes. I wondered where McKenna went. I also needed to see who was calling me.

Stopping by the restroom, I checked my phone and immediately called my brother back. Except it wasn't my brother who answered.

"Mom, why are you answering Derek's phone?"

"I'm with him, and he didn't want me to call you. He had a really bad patch today. I'm trying to persuade him to go to the hospital." My mother sounded on the verge of tears, but she was holding it together.

"Can you put him on the phone?" My mother's shaky breath came through the line in response. "Mom, I know how hard this is. I love you."

Her next breath was a little steadier. "I know you do, and I love you. Give me a sec. I'll see if he can talk."

I heard footsteps, followed by my mother's muffled voice. My brother got on the line a moment later. "Hey, man." His voice was thready.

"Hey, what's going on?"

"Bad timing for Mom to stop by."

"She's just checking on you."

"I know. I don't look good, so she wants to hurry me back to the hospital and get the doctor to try to change my mind about treatment."

"I know." My voice was clipped, and each beat of my heart was a dull, aching throb. "What can I do to help?"

"Nothing. I'm okay. Just a rough day. You sure you can handle me coming up there?"

"Absolutely." My voice was more confident than I felt. I didn't doubt that I could handle it, but I knew it would be brutally hard.

I heard our mother's voice in the background. "Do you want me to talk to her again?"

"I can handle it. I love you, man."

"Back atcha."

After we ended the call, I texted my mother. *I love you, and Derek loves you.*

At this moment, I wanted to run from my life. I didn't think I could handle going back into the winery for more small talk. When I stepped out into the hallway, I was relieved to see a server passing by. He took my empty bottle. I eyed both directions in the hallway, thinking it was going to be a pain in the ass to thread my way through the crowd in the front of the restaurant.

He thumbed the other direction. "Back door."

I followed where he pointed and slipped out into the darkness. I stopped for a minute once I was outside. The winter air was a bracing jolt.

Stuffing my hands in my pockets, I began walking. A moment later, I glanced ahead to see a silhouette turning onto the sidewalk. My pulse galloped faster. It was McKenna.

"McKenna!" My words were ahead of my brain, but it kicked in quick.

What the hell are you doing? You're not a good bet, not for someone like McKenna.

Shut up.

The list of reasons I wasn't a good bet for anyone for anything more than casual was pretty fucking long. Yet I didn't want to think about that now.

The air felt sharp and crisp as I began to jog. She didn't hear me call her name.

"Hey," I said when I reached her.

She jumped back and let out a startled gasp.

"Oh, hey, I didn't mean to startle you."

When I looked into her eyes, I saw raw fear flickering in the depths. Protectiveness rose inside me like a roar. I wanted to bundle her into my arms and make that fear disappear.

"Seriously." I reached a hand out to curl it over her shoulder. "I didn't mean to scare you." I could feel the subtle tremor in her body. "Are you okay?"

She blinked and looked away quickly. My hand fell away. It was beyond clear that she needed space. She curled her arms around her waist before she brought her eyes to mine again. "I'm fine. I guess I startle easily," she explained.

That was maybe an understatement. But then, maybe I was being an idiot. "Sometimes I can be a dumbass."

"What do you mean?

"It's dark, and you're walking alone down the sidewalk. I'm not worried about anything, but with the world we live in, most women don't want some guy appearing like that."

Her lips curved into sort of a smile, but it didn't reach her eyes. "I know you didn't mean any harm, Jack. It's just me."

I wanted to ask who hurt her, but now most definitely wasn't the time for that.

"Should I walk you home? Or are you parked somewhere nearby? Would you like me to go the other way and leave you alone?"

This time, her smile was a little more than the shape of her lips. "I'm guessing we're walking in the same direction."

"I think we are."

"In that case, please walk with me while I walk home." When she chuckled, the throaty sound zapped through me like a fiery sizzle.

McKenna reached into me, kicking away the compartment I'd tucked my heart inside. She made me want things I knew weren't sensible.

I must have delayed a little too long because she prompted, "Jack?"

"Let's walk together."

I fell into step beside her. We were quiet with nothing but the sound of our footsteps on the sidewalk. There were a few icy spots here and there, but she deftly dodged them.

She stopped in front of the harbor. "I love it here."

I glanced over. Electricity shimmered in the air like falling sparks around us. "Even growing up here, you still feel that way?"

She nodded. Together, we looked out over the harbor and beyond into the inky waters of the ocean. A half-moon rose over the mountains behind us, casting a pearly shimmer on the water.

"I do," she said, her tone almost reverent.

"You hear words like amazing, breathtaking, inspiring, and then you come to a place like this, and you *feel* those words," I offered.

I'd seen beautiful places and been in the wilderness before, but Alaska was unique. It felt like nature's cathedral. It snatched your breath out of your lungs. The world felt like so much more, with its beauty enough to wipe clean all the daily worries of life.

I felt McKenna glance toward me and slid my gaze to meet hers. It literally felt like sparks striking stone when our eyes collided, and heat shimmered in the air.

"It is like that." Her lips curled in a soft smile. "I'm glad you like it here."

"Like isn't adequate."

"No, it's not, is it?" she mused in a raspy whisper. There was a splash in the water. "Seal, probably."

"You can guess that in the darkness?"

She shrugged. "Things sound a certain way. Otters are a little messier and splashier in the water than seals."

"I bet you know all the best places."

She considered that before her smile widened. "I probably do. I can show you a few."

My heart surged in my chest. It wasn't just lust when it came to McKenna. Warmth curled through me like wisps of smoke.

"I'd like that."

She curled her arms around her waist again, shifting on her feet.

"Let's keep walking before you get too cold." I reflexively reached out, sliding my hand down her back in a coaxing touch. I was relieved when she didn't leap in fear this time.

When we began walking again, my hand fell away. I

wanted to hold her hand, to slide my thumb along the soft skin of her wrist, to feel her shiver from desire instead of cold.

She glanced sideways. "It's cold."

"A little," I teased in return.

A few minutes later, we turned off Main Street. As we approached her place, reluctance slowed my pace. We stopped in front of her house.

"Tell me something." She peered up at me.

"Anything."

A gust of wind whipped down the street and blew her hair in a little swirl. "What if..." She narrowed her eyes as she studied me.

The only light came from the glow of the lights on the porch. Her gaze was intent, and it felt as if she was trying to read into me while she tried to make a decision.

"What if we just—" She bluntly said, "I don't want a relationship."

"I don't either," I answered honestly.

"I want you."

At her words, need surged inside me like a fist pounding on the door, loud and insistent.

"I'd be lying if I said I didn't want you," I offered in the charged pause.

"What if we just had one night?"

Chapter Sixteen

MCKENNA

What if we just had one night?

I could *not* believe how bold I was.

Jack was silent. With every second that ticked by, I could hear the rush of blood in my ears as my heart pounded hard and fast. The air around us felt electric.

Just when I started to think I'd been far too reckless, his eyes locked on mine. "One night?"

With a swallow, I nodded.

"That's it?"

I blinked. Even though it felt physically impossible, my heart raced faster. "Well, it's a start." I collected myself. "I don't want things to get complicated."

"We agree on that. I'm not sure one night will be enough."

Just when I didn't know where to go with this conversation, he added, "But I'm not about to miss that one night. Your place or mine?"

With my pulse careening wildly, I gestured to my steps a few feet away before glancing down the street to his house. Although only two small houses separated mine and his, the distance between them seemed impossibly far. Right this very second, I needed what he was offering. I needed the escape.

Jack's hand closed around mine. It was warm, strong, and secure. A feeling I didn't expect.

I led him up the steps, stumbling a little on the top one. He released my hand, his palm landing on my hip as he steadied me. Everywhere he touched felt like lightning striking through me.

Thank goodness for force of habit and muscle memory. I managed to punch in the code to get into the house before we rushed through the door.

The living room area was dark, but I'd left a light on over the stove in the kitchen. It cast a soft glow in the background as I turned to look at him. The door clicked shut behind him, and quiet fell around us.

My eyes were instantly snagged in his intent blue gaze. He studied me soundlessly. "Are you sure about this?"

"I'm not sure about anything," I answered honestly. "But I want to kiss you again, and it's been a long day, and I want to forget."

"Forget what?"

Jack wasn't supposed to elicit this urge to confide. I wanted to tell him my secrets and let him hold and comfort me.

I shrugged. "I don't want to talk about it." Even if I was dodging, that was the truth.

I lifted a hand, placing it on his chest just above the zipper of his jacket. I hooked my finger over it, curling my knuckle as I dragged the zipper down. The sound was loud in the quiet room.

Jack never once looked away. When his jacket fell open, my hand dropped away. He took a step closer. It felt as if he was moving in slow motion, but then everything sped up. He unzipped my jacket, and his palms curled over my shoulders. The jacket slipped down behind me. He caught it with one hand, looping it over the coat rack by the door as he simultaneously shrugged out of his.

Seconds later, his palms landed on the door behind me, caging me between his arms. He was *right* there, inches away from me. My heart drummed, and heat blasted me from head to toe. His presence was strong and encompassing.

"One thing at a time," he said.

I took a shaky breath. "Okay," I rasped.

He dipped his head, dusting his lips over mine. It felt like a flame across my mouth. Heat prickled over the surface of my skin and spiraled through me. The air felt heavy, charged with electricity, as if just before a storm when thunder is rumbling, lightning is threatening, and the rain is about to break in a rush.

I made a pleading sound in the back of my throat. I was distantly surprised at it. I didn't usually want this much. I didn't usually even *feel* this much.

Jack had this disarming effect on me. All of my barriers fell away by the force of desire taking over.

I flexed upward to meet him as his mouth claimed mine. His lingering kiss was knee-weakening and melted me straight through. His tongue swept in masterful, devouring strokes. I was near frantic. One hand fisted his T-shirt, and the other slid around to grip his back. I needed something to hold on to.

By the time he lifted his head, we were both gasping for air. I sucked in deep breaths. My nipples were tight to the point of aching, and I could feel the moisture at the apex of my thighs. We stared at each other. A tiny corner of my mind registered that he looked as surprised as I felt.

"One thing at a time," he repeated.

I felt a brush against my ankles and glanced down to see Snowy, the kitten I'd scooped out of the cold, sidling up to our feet. Jack looked down, a laugh rustling in his throat.

"How's Snowy doing?"

It was just a simple question. Yet I experienced a little curl of warmth at discovering he remembered the name I'd bestowed upon the kitten.

"Good, I think. She's warm and dry and fed. She likes to scamper around and explore."

I pressed my palm on his chest, pushing him back. Snowy had already shown herself to be an independent girl, and with one more brush on my ankles, she walked over to the windows and leaped up, ignoring us in favor of the view outside.

Jack's lips curled in a smile. "She seems comfortable here."

"She is."

My knees barely held me up as I walked the few steps to my couch. All I knew was I needed something underneath me to keep me from melting to the floor.

We stopped in front of it, and Jack studied me for another beat. He lifted a hand, brushing my tangled hair away from my face before dipping his head and kissing me again. He took deep sips from my mouth as he cupped my cheeks. Even though I told myself this was nothing more than pure lust, just a freak of chemistry, I felt almost cradled by his touch.

Our hands began exploring. I stroked my palm over his chest, feeling along the hard-muscled planes. Another slipped around to trace up his back under the hem of his T-shirt. His skin was hot to the touch. All the while, I felt like pure fire, made of need and want.

"I need..." I began when I shoved his T-shirt up.

He reached up, catching his shirt just behind his neck and tugging it over in a quick swoop. My mouth went dry for a moment as I stared at him. He was fit, lean, and muscled, with a dusting of dark hair on his chest. I wanted more—to see more, to feel more, to touch more.

He turned, tracing his knuckle along the edge of my blouse. I wore an open blouse with a fitted long-sleeved T-shirt underneath. With a shimmy of my shoulders, I shrugged out of the blouse. His knuckles trailed down my sides, teasing under the curves of my breasts. My nipples practically begged for his touch.

Restless, with need driving me, I curled my hand on the hem of my shirt and lifted it up and over. Jack's nostrils flared as he looked at me. For a few seconds, I felt shy. I was a curvy girl with plump breasts and a soft, rounded belly. He opened his palm, unfurling it and sliding it over my belly and then up to caress one breast and then the other. Fire shimmered on my skin when I felt the brush of his lips along my collarbone while his thumb and forefinger pinched a nipple. I cried out sharply.

He lifted his head, then turned to sit on the couch. I moved on instinct, straddling him and sinking down over his hips. I simply... wanted.

Our next kiss felt like a bonfire, with his touch kindling the flames higher and higher inside. His hands slid over the curves of my hips before one palm shifted course, moving up my back in a smooth pass. The feel of his calloused palm sent hot sparks scattering over the surface of my skin.

It was hard to breathe. All I could manage to do was pant and suck in tiny gulps of air. Between the racing of my pulse and the need rushing through me, I craved release. Every touch fed into the gathering force of the fire like little flickers of oxygen, sending it higher and higher.

"McKenna," Jack rasped, his voice low and gruff.

It took an effort to drag my eyes open. We studied each other for a moment, the dim light from the kitchen catching the deep blue of his eyes. One of my palms was on his chest and the other curled around his muscled forearm.

I swallowed and swiped my tongue across my lips. "Yes?" I whispered.

His knuckles trailed down my breastbone, resting at the clasp of my bra. "May I?"

As if the question was even necessary. At my nod, I felt his thumb slide under the clasp. With subtle pressure, my bra fell open, and my breasts bounced free. I watched as his eyes darkened. He lightly cupped them both, his thumbs dragging in lazy strokes across the curves just under my nipples.

My nipples tightened to the point of pain. "Jack, I need—"

Thank God he could read my mind because he bent low and his mouth closed over a nipple. The subtle suction caused me to cry out sharply, my fingers spearing into his hair. He gave the same attention to my other nipple, lingering over them both before he leaned back.

"Fuck, McKenna," he rasped as his hand slid down over my waist.

"We could get to that," I managed to tease.

His chuckle sent a little shiver straight through me. "We could."

He rocked his hips just slightly, and I felt the friction of his arousal where it nestled against my core. My clit throbbed, the beat of my pulse pounding right there.

I scrambled off his lap to quickly shimmy out of my jeans. I needed to be bare against him and feel all of him. While I could've felt exposed under his gaze, which never once left me, I didn't.

I savored the feel of his eyes on me like a caress. My skin felt prickly. I was so desperate for more, so desperate for his touch. I was down to my panties when he said, "Wait."

I froze, one hand curled over the edge of the elastic. "For what?"

He reached for that hand, catching it and reeling me close until I stood between his knees. He shifted forward, dropping hot kisses on my belly while his thumb and finger squeezed one of my nipples. The sharp sensation arrowed straight to my core.

My pussy clenched, and I could feel the slick arousal there. "Jack," I pleaded.

He lifted his head, his eyes meeting mine as he dragged his palm almost lazily over the curve of my belly. He cupped it between my thighs, his fingers pressing lightly against the damp silk.

"What do you want, McKenna?"

We stared at each other. All I could hear was my heart pounding a thundering clap of need for him.

"You," I said simply.

His finger shifted, pushing the silk to the side and delving into my dripping core. I cried out, my hips rocking reflexively toward his touch. Once again, he took his time, teasing and exploring and barely coasting over my clit.

His fingers disappeared when I thought I couldn't stand it anymore. He dragged my panties down, and they fell around my ankles. I kicked them to the side. His touch was back where I needed it in a fiery second, sinking into me with two fingers and stretching my channel. It was a miracle I remained standing because I felt like liquid, made of need. For him.

He leaned forward, bringing his mouth to my sex. I thought maybe it was impossible, but there I stood as a man sat before me fucking me with his fingers and bringing me to a racing fast climax with his tongue and subtle suction on my clit.

Pleasure exploded, sizzling fast. I cried out, feeling myself clench around his fingers as pure sensation shattered through me. Just when my knees gave out, he caught me firmly and brought me back over his lap.

I felt the subtle crinkle of his hair against my skin as we looked at each other. I was stunned, awash in the aftershocks of pleasure.

"We can stop right now," he said.

"No way." My voice was low but clear. I needed more. I needed him inside me.

I reached between us, making quick work of the buttons on his fly even though my hands were rushed and almost clumsy. I glanced down when his cock sprang free as I shoved his boxers out of the way.

He shifted, moving his jeans down just enough. I curled my palm around his cock. It was warm, the skin velvety soft. I swiped over the drop of precum rolling out the top, lifting my thumb to lick it. His eyes darkened. Abruptly, he moved. "Condom."

I hadn't been thinking, not even barely. When he moved again, I savored the way the underside of his cock slid against my slippery, swollen clit, sending sharp streaks of pleasure through me.

Another moment later, he was rolling a condom on, protecting us both.

I rose up as he asked, "Are you sure?"

"Please," I responded.

I felt his crown pressing at my entrance, followed by the slow glide of him filling me. He was thick and long, and I was tight. It created the subtlest burn. I sank down slowly, shimmying my hips.

"Open your eyes," he ordered.

I would've done anything Jack asked me at this point. I dragged them open. I found his gaze waiting, hot and dark. I was restless. I shifted my hips slightly, but his palm curled on my hip to stop me. "Wait."

"What for?" I was pushy and impatient.

"Just a minute."

He lifted a hand, trailing his fingertips along my jawline. Goose bumps rose on my neck as his touch trailed down, teasing over my breasts and belly. I felt the press of his fingertips on my hips.

"Now," he said when his hips rocked up.

Chapter Seventeen

JACK

I dragged my eyes open, drawing in a deep breath and scrambling to maintain control. With McKenna clenching around me, I was awash in deeply intense pleasure.

"McKenna," I rasped.

Her lashes lifted. In the light cast from the kitchen, we stared at each other. Her entire body trembled. Her skin was silky and damp. Keeping one hand on her hip, I slid the other palm up her back, levering her forward just slightly.

I felt the soft give of her breasts against my chest, the tight points of her nipples. She smelled sweet with a salty hint. I dipped my head, breathing her in as I pressed lingering kisses along the side of her neck. I savored the way she shivered slightly and arched into me.

I relished every second of touching her, every subtle motion. Yet I was buying a little time, just enough to keep myself from pounding into her and finding my release in a blazing hot second.

She rocked her hips a little, and I lifted my head,

watching her face. She bit her bottom lip, and that was it. What little control I had snapped. I grabbed her hips, nudging into her deeper and deeper. She was slick and clenching around me, and my release was already threatening. My balls drew tight, and it felt as if an electric fire flickered at the base of my spine.

McKenna's teeth sank more deeply into her bottom lip as she rose up and sank down again. She was tight, so very tight around me. Once again, I had to reach deep for something, anything, to keep me from losing control before she did.

I leaned forward incrementally, bringing my mouth to hers in a messy kiss, nudging deeper with each rise and fall of her hips. I felt her begin to quicken again, her muscles tightening and her breath becoming shorter. Leaning back, I reached between us, bringing my fingers to where we were joined and circling them over her slippery, swollen clit.

I watched as her eyes fell closed, and she cried out sharply. Only then did I let go, my release cracking like lightning, hot and fierce. My mind blanked as the force of it surged through me.

We shuddered together, and I curled my arms around her to anchor myself, to hold her close as I gradually relaxed after the intense release.

Several moments later, she took a shaky breath, and I slowly loosened my arms as I leaned back into the couch. "McKenna," I whispered.

She opened her eyes. We studied each other for a moment before she shocked me. "Just so you know, technically, I was a virgin."

Chapter Eighteen

MCKENNA

...technically, I was a virgin.

Jack's expression shifted from relaxed to something neutral to shocked before his eyes narrowed. "What?"

I rolled my eyes. "It's no big deal. Virginity is just a social construct. I mean, technically."

"Technically? You just said you were *technically* a virgin. What exactly does that mean?"

I lifted one shoulder in a shrug. "It means that I've had plenty of experience fooling around. In the modern era, toys make things a little less of a big deal. I wasn't saving myself for anything, if that's what you're worried about."

Jack closed his eyes and took a slow breath. I sensed he was maybe confused by this. When he opened them again, he was quiet for several beats. Although my pulse had been working overtime for the last hour or so, it picked up the pace again. I regretted saying anything. To be honest, I didn't know why I did.

"I shouldn't have mentioned it. It's really not a thing."

"What do you mean by social construct?"

"It was originally turned into an issue, a construct for men, a way to ensure they could confirm paternity. They linked that to women's purity. This whole thing about the hymen is a joke. You don't even have to have intercourse or..." I tried to formulate my thoughts.

"Use a vibrator," Jack interjected helpfully.

When a giggle slipped out, I was relieved to see the tiniest hint of a smile when his lips curled up at one corner.

"Yes. Anyway, for some reason, I decided to mention it to you."

"Why me?"

That question made me squirm inside just a little bit. I shrugged again. "I'm not sure."

I was hedging a little, and I knew it. The truth was the chemistry I had with Jack was something I'd never experienced before. I'd given up on ever experiencing anything like that. I'd given up so thoroughly that I'd convinced myself it wasn't even a possibility.

My response to Jack had me rethinking some of my past assumptions. For example, I had concluded you could maybe get a fluttery belly, and your pulse could race, but it didn't always mean anything. Sometimes you felt the feelings, but then you kissed someone, and it wasn't all that great. The chemistry fizzled into nothing but smoke and mirrors.

With Jack, every touch, every look, every moment with him just amped up the feelings. But I wasn't about to go into all of that with him. That was far more than I wanted to share. Contemplating it, I felt vulnerable and unsure.

Jack pressed his tongue into his cheek. "I think

there's more to the story, and maybe someday you'll decide you trust me enough to tell me."

I opened my mouth to argue the point as my cheeks heated. Maybe I would trust him enough to tell him. Right now, trust wasn't something that came easy.

I didn't know how, but I dredged up some composure.

Chapter Nineteen

JACK

McKenna stood in front of me with one foot curled over the other. She wore bright blue socks paired with leggings and a fleece sweatshirt that hung below her hips. Her hair was a tousled mess, and her gray-blue eyes were bright. Her skin was still flushed.

"Did you even eat?" Her voice punctured the haze in my mind.

After my electrifying encounter with her, my mind was still blown by her startling statement. Intellectually speaking, I understood her point. Maybe I'd never studied up on the social context around virginity, but it made sense. I realized it didn't have to be a big deal. Hell, there was nothing glorious about when I lost my virginity. I'd been a senior in high school, and Jenny had been the prettiest girl in the universe ever to me. She'd unceremoniously stomped on my heart when she dumped me a month later for another guy. Oh, to be that young again.

Somehow, inside of a single hour, things had gone beyond just fooling around with McKenna. The situation felt as if it was barreling out of my control. All things considered, she was probably smart to stick with toys. I came with messy, emotional complications. For me, there was also a firm boundary about not getting involved. I had other worries. A job that wasn't safe and took me away for stretches of time, and a sick brother who was going to come live with me until he died. I didn't have the bandwidth for any kind of emotional complication.

"Jack?" she prompted.

What the hell had she asked me? Oh right. "I didn't eat," I finally said. "Why do you ask?"

McKenna waggled her brows, her eyes tilting up at the corners with her smile. "Because your stomach just growled. I didn't eat either. Let's order some pizza."

Maybe McKenna wasn't my first, but I experienced a first with her. I didn't want to just get the hell out of here. After my last serious relationship ended when my ex declared she assumed I'd change my mind about wanting kids (spoiler alert: I still didn't want kids), I kept scrupulous boundaries. Usually, I was in a rush to make sure there was no confusion, and a part of that meant not spending too much time together. But with McKenna, I wanted to stay. Beyond the fact that she was sexy, delectable, and cute, I liked being around her. I wanted to linger in her presence, and it wasn't about sex.

Without thinking, I nodded. She declared pepperoni to be her favorite, and I wasn't about to dispute that point. There was nothing like a good pepperoni pizza. She lifted her phone to dial and hesitated before saying, "Fuck it."

After she quickly called in our order, I asked, "Fuck what?"

"I wasn't going to order from Fireweed Winery even though it's the best pizza in town, and I'm not just being biased. But I don't want to waste money on so-so pizza. The only other place is the grocery store deli, which is good in a pinch, but that's about it."

"Is there a problem with ordering from the winery?"

She gestured for me to sit on one of the stools by her kitchen island. "Not really. It's just if the delivery driver feels like gossiping, they might mention to someone in the family that you were here tonight."

I chuckled. "Ah, the unintended consequences of living in a small town."

"And having a nosy family and too many siblings."

I mentally counted. "There are seven of you?"

McKenna's lips twisted to the side in a lopsided grin, but something dark flickered in her eyes. "There are seven of us, and I'm the youngest and the only girl." She paused, a mix of emotions crossing her face before she added, "Our oldest brother Jake died from alcohol poisoning in college."

"Oh. I'm really sorry." Those words felt inadequate, but that was all there was to say.

"Thank you. You'll hear about it around town. Gossip is a thing in small towns, and Fireweed Harbor is no exception. I try to ignore it most of the time, but I know there are rumors about our family."

I nodded after a beat. "I can imagine. Aside from the usual small-town chatter, you all own an international corporation. I heard someone describe your family as Fireweed Harbor royalty."

McKenna rolled her eyes at that. "Trust me, we're not royalty. Unless you count the messy family history." She didn't seem to want to talk further.

"Is there any family that isn't messy?" I commented lightly.

Her expression was soft as she looked at me. "I suppose not. But when it's yours, it feels so big."

"Absolutely."

"How many siblings do you have, if any?"

She couldn't have known just how loaded that question was. I had practice with keeping my emotions in check. "Just one. My brother."

"Older or younger?"

"Derek's older." I took a breath, steeling myself. "By one year. We've always been close. I'm in a hurry to buy my own place because my brother is sick. He has nonsmoker's lung cancer from exposure to radon gas. He's dying. He's had three rounds of treatment and doesn't want to go through another."

McKenna's hand flew to her chest just as she began to open the refrigerator. She turned back to face me. "Oh no! I am so sorry."

I ignored the stinging sensation in my heart and swallowed through the knot aching in my throat as I took in a slow, careful breath. "Thank you. He's coming up here as soon as he can. We have family in Diamond Creek and have visited over the years. We've both always loved Alaska. When I took this job, and he found out the cancer was back, he asked if he could come stay with me. I want to fix it, and I can't."

McKenna looked at me quietly. "I can imagine. You seem like a fix-it kind of guy." Her words were soft and understanding.

"I can't fix this, and I hate it. I imagine you would do the same for one of your brothers."

She nodded without hesitation. "If there's anything I can do—" Her words cut off abruptly before she pursed her lips. "I like to fix things too, and there's really nothing I can do to fix this, but I'll help if you need anything."

"I appreciate that. You know what it's like to lose a brother."

Something flickered in her gaze, something like sadness. It felt as if she wanted to say more. At that moment, the doorbell rang, the sound snapping through the moment. McKenna practically jumped out of her skin at the sound. She blinked. "I'll get that."

I reached for my wallet, only to discover it wasn't even in my pocket. "I can cover it," I offered as I stood. My wallet had to have fallen onto the sofa in the midst of our heated encounter when I was fumbling for a condom.

She waved me away and walked briskly toward the front door. "Family gets a deal for pizza."

Moments later, the pizza was spread out on the counter, and McKenna sat across from me. I shouldn't have been distracted by the sight of her eating. She was just eating. But I happened to look up right after she finished a slice of pizza. She swallowed, and her tongue darted out to the corner of her mouth before she dabbed at her lips with a napkin.

My nerves sizzled with fire. Fuck me.

Beyond the burning need I felt when I was with her, I found the more time I spent with McKenna, the more I liked her. It was easy to talk with her. I'd surprised myself by telling her about my brother.

As if she could read my mind, she asked, "So when will your brother be moving here?"

"I'm scheduled to close on the house next month." I glanced at my watch. "Which is why it worked out for me to find a short-term rental like I mentioned before. Once I move in, I'll have to do a few things to make sure it's set up for him, and then he'll move here."

"What do you need to do?"

"Not much. I need for the house to be accessible and so on. He can walk on his own, but he's pretty weak, so I want to make sure it's comfortable. It's a single-story home, so it's pretty easy to manage."

McKenna looked worried. Her brow furrowed, and her teeth sank into the bottom corner of her lip. "I want to give you all kinds of suggestions for medical options in Juneau."

"Trust me, I'm full of suggestions for my brother. He's already done all the things. He's had world-class medical care, three rounds of treatment, and then some. He just wants to be comfortable. I've already been in touch with the hospital here. His medical team down there is coordinating to ensure he can have palliative care when it's time." I paused as my heart thumped with an ache that got sharper as time passed.

"Would you change anything if you could?" she asked, her tone soft.

"Of course. I wish he wasn't this sick. I wish a lot of things, but that's where we're at. It's his call, not mine. I do understand. I was with him during his last round of treatment, and it was brutal. He was so miserable. I've never had cancer, but what I saw is nothing I'd want to experience. The doctors have said the odds aren't good."

As McKenna held my gaze, my heart eased a little. While I was caught in the undercurrent of pain and sadness for what my brother was experiencing and the loss I knew was coming, I sensed she understood.

A few moments passed while we ate before she asked, "Do you want to keep talking about this?"

"Of course not. I don't mean that I mind you asking, but it's hard. I know it's coming, and I'm there for him."

"Okay."

"Tell me about what it's like to grow up with so many brothers."

Her lips pressed together before she let out a muffled snort. "It's something all right," she said dryly. "I grew up with seven, lost one, and then we learned we had an older half-brother a few years ago. Fortunately, he's awesome." She paused before lifting her hands and letting them fall. "It's complicated and I'm not even joking."

I chuckled. "I can imagine. My brother usually feels like he has a say in my life, and there's just one of him."

She grinned. "I do the same to them. It's just a different dynamic. At times, I wished I was an only child and still do. But then, I also wouldn't trade it for anything. We haven't always had it easy."

"It must've been hard to lose your older brother," I offered.

She studied me quietly. "It was, it is. But..." She shrugged. I sensed there were a lot of tangles in that answer.

"And there we go talking about hard things again," she said softly.

"Should we talk about the weather?" I teased lightly.

She laughed, the throaty sound sending a fiery sizzle through me.

"Well, you moved here smack in the middle of winter. Speaking of weather, I hope you don't mind the cold and snow."

"Not at all. I've always loved snow. We lived in the foothills of the Cascades, so I'm used to some snow. Maybe not as much as you get here."

"Do you like to ski? Your family owns that ski lodge in Diamond Creek, right?"

I nodded. "I do like to ski, both downhill and cross-country. What about you?"

Not much later, McKenna was putting away plates and tucking the leftover pizza in the box. She glanced over at me after she closed the refrigerator door.

"Do you want to stay or go?"

Chapter Twenty

MCKENNA

As soon as I asked the question, I silently cursed to myself. By asking, I put it out there that I wanted him to stay. I did, *so* very much. But what if he didn't want to stay? Cue the awkward moment.

My charged question lingered in the air between us. I could feel the echo of my heartbeat reverberating against my rib cage. I didn't realize I was holding my breath until Jack nodded.

"Stay," he said.

My breath released in a whoosh.

———

Something woke me, maybe a gust of wind against the windows. I was curled up on my side. I felt warm, comfortable, and protected. Jack was spooned behind me.

I blinked my eyes open to see the clock on my nightstand read 5:30 a.m. I usually woke up around six. I took a soft breath, savoring the warmth.

With Jack, every expectation was being proven wrong.

His knees were tucked in the bend of mine, and I could feel his muscled body curled behind me, relaxed in sleep. One arm was draped along my hip with his palm resting on the curve of my belly. I savored the touch. It felt so good to be held.

My mind spun back to last night and his look of surprise when I explained I'd technically been a virgin. I almost snorted aloud as I lay there. I hadn't wanted it to mean much. It was a pesky detail.

When I took another breath, I felt Jack come awake. His palm shifted, and his thumb stroked along the edge of my waist.

"McKenna?" His voice was rumbly and gruff.

The sound of my name sent a shiver through my whole body. "Yes?"

"Are you awake?"

Chapter Twenty-One

MCKENNA

Tessa and Quinn were already there when I walked into the restaurant at Fireweed Winery. Some people assumed I ate here regularly because it was my family's restaurant. Don't get me wrong, I *was* loyal, but I ate here because the food was freaking amazing. It was so good we landed in world-class curated restaurant reviews more than once.

The hostess glanced up and waved me by when I walked in. "Your friends already got a table."

Tessa smiled up at me when I approached.

"Hey!" Quinn lifted her wineglass aloft.

"We already got drinks," Tessa added.

"What did you get me?" I slipped into my chair after hanging my jacket on the back.

"I'm in the mood for wine," Quinn replied, "but Tessa is in the mood for a mellow gooseberry mead."

Tessa gestured back and forth between the bottles. "Take your pick."

"Is Fiona still meeting us?"

Quinn took a swallow of her wine as she nodded. "I came through the back, and she walked in with me.

I tried to keep her from checking on the specials, but—"

Tessa rolled her eyes, finishing Quinn's sentence. "She can't help herself."

"I'm here!" Fiona said over my shoulder.

"So if they had enough time to order wine, you were checking on the specials for a few minutes," I chimed in as Fiona slipped into the chair beside me.

When her cheeks turned pink, I waggled my brows. "Oh, Blake's working late."

Tessa's chuckle was sly when Quinn offered, "Make-out session with the hubs."

Fiona grabbed the glass of ice water in front of her and took a long swallow before shrugging. "I was just saying hi."

"I don't need to know anything about any of my brothers making out in the office." I cast a faux glare between Quinn and Fiona. With Quinn married to Kenan and Fiona married to Blake, I was grateful that I had sisters-in-law I loved, but I had to set some boundaries.

"You don't have to worry about that with me," Tessa offered, brushing her auburn curls off her shoulders.

I filled my glass with mead. "Tessa and I have solidarity."

"Solidarity?" Fiona prompted. She was the newest friend in our circle, having moved to Fireweed Harbor only two years prior.

"I've already been married and divorced. I have a son and a custody battle for at least the next fifteen years," Tessa said. "I will *never* be in another committed relationship."

"Oh." That was Fiona's only response to the bitterness laced within Tessa's words.

"Trust me, she has good reasons," I offered with a nod toward Tessa. "At least you're divorced now."

"Exactly, but what about you?" Tessa prompted.

"What do you mean?" I countered. "I don't want to get serious." I had a pat answer whenever this came up. "I don't think there's anything wrong with just wanting to enjoy life on my own. I have a big family. I'll be everyone's favorite aunt."

Quinn cut in. "The only aunt. All of your siblings are brothers."

Tessa snorted.

"Fine. Just, that's it. I don't want the pressure."

"But what if you fall in love?" Fiona asked softly.

"I won't."

"I admire your confidence," Quinn said. She paused, studying me. "I didn't think I would ever fall for anyone."

"That's because you weren't paying attention to Kenan. You two were best friends, and it took years for you to figure out you were perfect together," I offered.

Quinn shrugged, unperturbed by my observation. "You really don't know what's going to happen. Life can surprise you."

"I didn't think I would ever be serious with anyone again," Fiona chimed in. She tended to be somewhat solemn, and I liked that about her. She conveyed a sense of quiet strength.

I looked at Tessa. "You understand."

She rolled her eyes. "Oh, I do, but I'm not sure why you feel this way."

I didn't care to explain. I didn't even remember my own father. I'd been too young to remember when he died. I had to watch our grandfather terrorize all of us after our dad died and wonder why nobody protected us. I became my oldest brother's target, while he was the primary target for our grandfather. Those lessons had been important. I knew things could look a certain way on the outside and be entirely different behind closed doors.

I did what I usually did and played this off with a shrug. "I don't have to have a good reason. When it comes to being a woman in the world, the cards are not marked in our favor. No matter how far we've come, it's a man's world. Look at what's happening now. They're trying to take away the rights we've won."

"That's a depressing point," Quinn said as the server arrived to check on us.

After he took our orders and left, I glanced at Fiona. "Poor guy is totally nervous having you here."

"It's not just me. You're here," she pointed out.

"We'll leave a good tip for his stress."

We were in the midst of our main course when I heard my brother Wyatt's voice. I glanced over to see him leaning on the corner of the bar, not too far from our table. The bartender handed him a bottle before he headed our way.

Since my brief interaction with him the other night, I felt a deeper kinship with Wyatt. He knew about the unwanted baggage tangled around me.

"Are you joining us?" I asked when he stopped beside my shoulder.

"No, just saying hi. I'm meeting with Adam and Blake to discuss the details about taking over as the head brewer here."

As if on cue, Adam came through the side door behind the bar and made a beeline for us.

"Your timing is perfect," Quinn offered with a grin.

"No Kenan?" Fiona prompted just as Adam stopped beside Wyatt.

Adam chimed in, "He's meeting us too, last-minute addition." He glanced toward Quinn. "He said you left him alone for the night."

I let out a laugh at the twinkle in Adam's eyes.

Quinn shrugged. "He'll survive."

Wyatt placed his hand on my shoulder, the casual squeeze reassuring. My brothers departed, and I happened to be glancing toward Tessa and noticed her gaze practically burning holes in Adam's back.

I wasn't thinking when I asked, "Uh, what did Adam do to you?"

Tessa snapped her eyes to me. "Nothing."

I didn't know what undercurrent I was missing, but clearly, I needed to get up to speed.

A short while later, we had finished paying when Blake and Kenan came out and swooped in to depart with Quinn and Fiona.

As we all stood beside the table for a moment, putting on our jackets, I glanced from one couple to the next. My eyes collided with Tessa's. She looked as resigned as I felt. I was happy for my brothers, truly. Yet I couldn't imagine having the kind of love they'd found.

A tiny voice in my thoughts piped up in a high-pitched whisper. *There's Jack.*

My far more developed cynical voice retorted quickly. *Jack is hot. He's pretty nice, but that's it. Don't go wishing for things you can't have.*

I said my goodbyes and turned to walk home. The night air was crisp and icy cold, and my boots crunched on the sidewalk. It was clear of snow with a few icy patches. The rock salt on the road and side-walk glittered under the moon and streetlights.

I had a habit of going to the harbor docks whenever I walked at night. It was beautiful and felt both invigorating and soothing. As I strolled along the docks, I could feel the movement of the water underneath and hear the soft lap of the water slapping against the sides of the boats. I took a breath, savoring the salty air. I looked up at the dark mountain ridges forming a jagged line in the night sky, the moon behind them glittering on the inky-black water in the quiet town.

I stuffed my hands in my pockets, shivering slightly as I turned to look from the harbor toward town. My hometown was nestled into the foothills of the mountains. The winding roads were illuminated by the lights from houses.

I started walking home, my hair blowing in a spin. A moment later, I let out a startled squeak when footsteps approached.

"It's just me, McKenna." Jack's voice reached me as I turned back to see him.

I took an unsteady breath. "Oh." He stopped beside me. I didn't like being startled. Not at all. "Where did you come from?"

"I was just coming out of the grocery store." He gestured to the store at an angle across from us on the other side of the street.

"Oh."

I felt a little silly, maybe a lot silly, but I didn't suppose I could do anything about my startle reflex.

"I'll have to remember it's easy to scare you. I didn't mean to."

I looked up at him, trying to tell myself that my heart had taken off like a horse out of the gate at a race because he startled me. Maybe that was what started it, but it wasn't slowing. Three entire nights had passed since my night with him. I wanted to lie and tell myself I hadn't thought about him. My thoughts had turned to him during any moment when I wasn't preoccupied.

"Can I walk you home?"

We strode through the quiet darkness. My entire body hummed with a subtle electricity. I told myself that Jack was just accompanying me home and that there was nothing more to it.

Because I don't want anything more. Right?

We stopped in front of my steps. *Just say good night.*

When I looked up at him and felt the heat on my cheeks, I hoped it was too dark for him to notice.

"Do you want to come in?"

When Jack hesitated and looked away, I took a breath and ignored the rush of disappointment.

"Yes, but you need to know something."

"What's that?"

Chapter Twenty-Two

JACK

Against my better judgment, we stood outside of McKenna's house. The air had a bite of icy cold to it.

When McKenna shivered a little, curling her shoulders forward, I reflexively reached for her. "Maybe we could talk inside?"

A moment later, she was slipping out of her coat. "Let me turn up the heat," she said as she kicked off her boots. She padded across the living room to the thermostat by the bathroom door.

"Do you want to start a fire?"

"Sure, you just—" She began when I walked over to the switch by the fireplace.

"Turn this on," I offered with a wink. The propane flames flickered on.

She grinned just as Snowy leaped down from the top of the refrigerator. McKenna leaned down to pet her before the kitten made her way over to inspect me. When I stroked her back, a purr rumbled from her throat. She didn't dally, though, and meandered over to the windows overlooking the street and hopped up to sit on the windowsill.

"Snowy loves it there," McKenna offered. "She likes watching anything that moves."

"Most cats do."

"Do you want anything to drink?" she asked.

"Are you having anything?"

She opened her refrigerator, peering inside. "Maybe. I have juice, water, and honey blueberry mead. No beer."

"If you're having mead, I'll take some."

McKenna approached the living room a moment later, handing me a bottle. "Sit." She gestured to the couch.

"I'll have to find some of my own furniture when I move into my house," I commented. "Don't suppose you'll let me take the furniture with me."

She chuckled as she shook her head.

"I love these couches. They're seriously comfortable."

"I can tell you exactly where we get them. I'll have Sandy let you know."

"The Sandy who was on vacation when I looked at my place?"

"That's the one."

"That would be great. I just want comfortable furniture, and I hate shopping."

"Can't say I blame you," McKenna replied with a quick smile.

"Why are you in one of your family's rentals?" I couldn't help my curiosity.

McKenna took a swallow of her mead, temporarily distracting me. My gaze lingered on her lips as she drew the bottle away. Her tongue slid across her delectable bottom lip before she replied, "We relocated the headquarters for Fireweed Industries back here only a few years ago. I handle public relations, so

I was in Seattle. We've always had the winery, the brewery, and the restaurant here. I just haven't gotten around to sorting out whether I want to build or buy a place. My mother, of course, offered to let me stay in the house where we grew up, but—" Her lips twisted to the side, and she shrugged. "I love my mother, but I want my own space." She swept a hand in an arc. "These houses are nice."

"I completely understand. If it weren't that I needed a place for my brother to be with me, I would probably happily stay in one of these."

McKenna leaned forward and set her bottle on the coffee table. "You said you wanted to explain something."

She faced me fully. The desire I felt for her was an ever-present distraction. When she lifted her hand, her fingers absently fiddling with one of the buttons on her silky blouse, I wanted to lean over and drag my tongue along her skin.

I forced my attention away. "I want you," I said.

Pink crested high on McKenna's cheeks. "That's what you wanted to talk to me about?"

"After the other night..." I tried to corral my competing urges into a sensible path forward. As I stared into McKenna's pretty eyes, I had to face reality. Nothing about my reaction to McKenna or what she made me want was sensible.

Still, I forced myself to forge ahead. "I don't want you to get the wrong idea. I feel like I need to be straightforward about the fact that my life doesn't have room for a relationship. Once my brother's here, I'll be focused on him. Beyond that, my job isn't convenient for anything like a relationship."

Her eyes narrowed. "Did I give you the impression I wanted a relationship?"

Her blunt comment knocked me mentally off balance for a beat. "No, but I actually like you. I don't want to be an asshole, even by accident. Beyond my life right now, I've never wanted to have kids. That seems like something many people want."

"I don't." McKenna's reply was sharp and clear.

I sensed hints of anger and pain underneath her words.

"Okay."

We were quiet for a few beats before McKenna leaned forward, reaching for her bottle of mead and taking a long swallow before setting it down. "Is that it, then?" she asked.

I felt like this conversation hadn't gone the way I intended and tried to correct the course. "McKenna, the other night was incredible. I don't want it to be—"

She cut in swiftly. "We can just leave it at one night." The expression on her face was carefully flat.

Disappointment sliced through me. Even if I was busy reminding myself I wasn't a good bet, that I didn't have time for anything else, it hurt more than I expected for her to so easily insist one night was all we would have.

Before I could think better of it, I spoke. "I don't just want one night." There was a force behind my words, surprising me with its intensity.

McKenna blinked, her eyes widening slightly. I reached for her hand, where it rested on her knee, and turned it over in mine. Lifting it, I dusted a kiss on the inside of her wrist. Her breath hissed through her teeth. The sound of her swallowing was loud in the charged space between us.

"Oh."

"Is that all you want? Just one night? Because I want more than one more time with you, and I have a feeling that won't be enough." Me, the bad bet, the guy who never wanted anyone to expect anything, was fighting for more than a one-night stand.

She shook her head but didn't say anything.

"Does that mean you don't want one more night, or you *do* want more?"

The flush on her cheeks deepened. "That's not all I want."

"Tell me why you don't want to have a relationship." My curiosity got the best of me.

Wariness flickered in her eyes before she shrugged casually. "I just don't see why it's such a big deal for everyone. That's all."

"Is that really all?" I pressed.

You're sure asking a lot of questions, my cynical mind taunted me.

I sure was.

"That's all that matters," she said tartly.

It said something about just how bad I had it for this woman that I considered that a win, that she even admitted there might be something more.

While I didn't offer more, I couldn't imagine letting my heart be open to anyone, not when my brother was dying, not when my job didn't leave room for more. That's what I always told myself.

"So what are we doing?" Her question landed in the space between us like a lit fuse.

"We've agreed that neither one of us wants anything serious. And we're neighbors." She circled her hand in the air impatiently when I paused to consider my words. "We're going to have more then. Do we need to discuss anything further?"

A corner of my mind thought this was ridiculous as if we were having some kind of rational discussion when all I wanted was to be buried inside her.

McKenna shook her head. Before I could think, she leaned forward and brought her lips to mine. The soft press of her lips was a fiery shock to my system.

Maybe my doubts banged around inside my mind, but my body knew exactly what it wanted. Instinct took over the moment her lips teased against mine.

I shifted closer, giving a subtle tug on her hand. Seconds later, she was a bundle of softness on my lap. She made this sweet little sound in the back of her throat. It was like being struck by lightning, the sound itself sizzling down my spine with sparks leaping in its wake. Our kiss went from a languid, sensual exploration to devouring with our teeth banging together at one point. We broke apart, staring at each other, wide-eyed and shocked at the power of the combustion between us. It had a life of its own.

"McKenna," I rasped. Her name slipped out unbidden.

She started to move, but her knee banged into the coffee table, sending her half-empty bottle of mead tumbling over. "Oh hell!" She stood swiftly.

She hurried into the kitchen, returning with paper towels. I carried the bottle to the sink and rinsed it while she wiped up the spill. A moment later, she stood beside me in the kitchen, tossing the paper towels into the garbage under the sink before rinsing her hands.

My heart had barely even slowed from its rampaging beat. She looked up at me.

Seconds ticked by. It was as if there was a clock in my body. Too much time had passed since we'd kissed even though it'd maybe been two minutes.

She stepped closer, her eyes lifting to mine as she placed a palm on my chest. Her touch was electric. I considered myself a deeply practical person. Chemistry was chemistry; kissing was kissing. It felt good and was simply a convenient attunement of pheromones.

Yet McKenna made me question just how practical I really was. Because this chemistry with her was like nothing I had *ever* encountered. It felt like capturing lightning from the sky and spinning it around us, like a burning fire when the wind catches in it.

I dipped my head, letting my forehead fall to hers just as she asked, "Where were we?"

"Right here, sweetheart." My last word was the beginning of our kiss. I cupped both of her cheeks, angled my head to the side, and let my need take over. It was a rushing force, a river breaking through a dam in spring and obliterating anything in its path.

McKenna's palms mapped my chest, one sliding down and stroking boldly over the aching length of my cock. I groaned into our kiss before I broke away and sucked in a deep breath. We stared at each other, the air so charged it felt like it might catch fire.

Her deft and swift hands unbuttoned my fly. The zipper sliding down fed into the electricity sizzling through me.

Another moment later, I gritted my teeth and let out a growl. Her bare palm slid into my boxers. Her touch was sure, and I clung to the thinnest thread of control. I ached. I scrambled mentally for purchase, something to hold onto to regain control.

She slid her thumb over the tip of my cock, lifting her hand. I could feel the beat of my heart in my swollen length when her lips closed around her thumb, and she moaned a little.

My voice was tight when I bit out, "McKenna."

She bit the corner of her lips. The next thing I

knew, she leaned down to shove my boxers out of the way as my cock sprang free.

I felt her mouth close over the tip of my cock, her tongue swirling as she created a subtle suction. Burying my fingers in her hair, I held on, letting myself savor every second of this.

She teased me, her tongue lazily circling before sliding down along the underside of my cock and up again. She drew me into her mouth, bringing me in deep. I felt the curl of her palm around the base of my cock when she drew away. I nearly cried out. My release threatened, sizzling hot at the base of my spine as my balls drew tight.

"McKenna," I gasped.

She rocked back on her heels. "Yes?" Her lips were glistening and puffy.

I wanted to come inside her, but I couldn't even manage to say anything.

"Too late," she added.

I felt the warm suction of her mouth closing around my length again. My grip tightened on her hair as she drew me deep inside. Heat blasted me in a fiery jolt before my release spurted into her mouth.

It was a damn good thing I had a counter behind me because my knees nearly gave out from the force.

Chapter Twenty-Three

JACK

One hand curled against the counter, and I forced myself to loosen the grip of my fingers on her hair. McKenna released me, her eyes dark as she slowly rose to stand again.

My heartbeat echoed through my body as I stared at her. She placed her palm on my chest. My heart lunged, kicking toward the warmth of her touch.

Gulping in a deep breath, I pulled myself together. "I need you." My voice was gruff, a ragged whisper as I reached for her. "I need more."

I slid an arm around her waist. Everything felt as if it were melting together. One kiss blurred into the next. She was soft and warm. The relief that came from my climax was quickly replaced with a fire, burning hotter and higher between us with every touch, like throwing another match into the bonfire.

I was impatient and restless when I reached between her thighs. She rocked her hips against my palm, the motion whipping the need burning hotter and faster. I groaned against the sweet skin of her neck when I nipped lightly while one hand was busy sliding her zipper down.

McKenna stepped back, shimmying out of her jeans. I spun her around. It was a fumbled rush as I slid her hips onto the counter. I pressed her knees apart to look down and see the very heart of her. Her pussy was pink, her folds plump and glistening with her arousal. Her breath was coming in heaves when I lifted my eyes to hers.

"Your turn," I murmured before I gave her a hard kiss.

Breaking free, I slid my fingers into her folds, teasing at her entrance with a lazy circle. I watched her as her lashes dropped. She bit her lip, letting out something between a whimper and a moan.

I lifted my fingers and drew them into my mouth, tasting the salty tang of her desire. She let out a ragged breath before I leaned forward, blowing lightly over her sex.

"Jack..." Her tone was pleading.

I blew again, and her legs trembled where my palms rested on the insides of her thighs. On the heels of another breath, I brought my mouth to her. Her fingers speared my hair, and she cried out, her hips bucking roughly against me. I savored her, taking my sweet time. I lazily explored her with my tongue, barely glancing over her clit again and again until I felt the sting on my scalp from her gripping my hair.

"Jack, please."

I drew back, lifting my eyes to look at her. "Please, what?" I drawled.

Her eyes opened. "Make me come."

Holding her gaze, I sank two fingers inside her, watching as her hips rocked forward and feeling the clench of her pussy.

Her breath was ragged. "Please..."

"Okay, sweetheart." I brought my mouth to her sex again, circling her swollen clit just before I sucked on it lightly.

Her cry was sharp and keening, her body trembling and tight. I stayed with her until she began to relax. I leaned back, straightening slowly.

I was nearly desperate to feel her again. I stood between her thighs. We were both half-dressed. Her, with her shirt still on and hanging open. Me, with my shirt on the floor and my jeans hanging open. My cock jutted out with cum rolling out the tip and down along the underside.

It was hard to believe she had brought me to release only moments earlier. That was how much I needed her.

She reached between us, curling her palm around my cock. I *had* to kiss her. Bringing my mouth to hers, I could taste the mingle of her arousal and mine. Our kiss was open, slow, and deep. When we broke apart, our gazes locked.

I was just about to curl my palm around my cock and fill her when reality shouted out from the distant recesses of my mind. "Fuck, I need a condom."

McKenna curled her legs around my hips before I could step back. "I have an IUD."

I trusted her. But I was frantically religious about protection. "Are you sure?"

"Am I sure I have an IUD, or am I sure I want you to fuck me? Yes, to both." She paused after that blunt statement sent a shot of blood straight to my aching cock. "If you need to get a condom, please do."

I couldn't help but chuckle. "If you're sure, I'm sure." I stepped closer.

I shifted, bringing her hips closer to the edge of

the counter. Reaching between us, I positioned my cock at her entrance. We looked down together. I let out a low groan as I filled her slowly, watching as her pussy lips stretched open. It was intensely arousing. I lifted my eyes to hers. "You feel so good," I slurred.

"You do too," she whispered.

Only moments earlier, we had an entire conversation about how this was just essentially friends with benefits. Yet I could feel something else shimmying to life between us, a deeply intimate feeling I had never experienced with anyone.

We looked down together again as I slid my hips back, watching until I was seated fully inside her. I slid an arm around her waist, cupping her cheek with my other palm as I began to fuck her slow and deep.

I felt surrounded, encompassed—by Jack. He rocked into me in slow nudges. My legs hung down with my feet hooked loosely around his thighs. The angle created an intense friction right where we were joined. Every time he filled me, sharp little bursts of pleasure radiated outward through my body. The intense orgasm he'd brought me to with his mouth was rolling into another.

My body felt liquid, melting with need and pleasure twining together. All the while, he fucked me, each thrust a little deeper than the last. The pressure building inside was almost unbearable. I toed the edge of release until everything drew tight and then broke apart, shattering me with its force. I cried out into our kiss. He pulled back slightly, his forehead resting on mine as he said, "Let go, sweetheart."

He held me tight while I spun wild. I felt him following me into the storm when he cried out sharply, and I could feel the warmth of his release filling me. We shuddered together. I tucked my head into the curve of his neck, curling close as he held me. I felt cherished.

For all of my internal tough talk, that I never wanted anything serious, that I couldn't trust anyone enough to be vulnerable, I felt the hard shell around my heart softening and the cracks spreading.

As we disentangled ourselves, I gave myself a little lecture.

Just put on your clothes and tell him good night. It doesn't have to be a big deal. It's nothing more than amazing sex.

My mouth was ahead of my brain. "Do you want to stay?"

Chapter Twenty-Five

JACK

Six weeks later

"You outdid yourself," my brother said.

I glanced over from where I stood at the kitchen counter in our new house. I cracked a grin, calling over my shoulder, "You know I like to overachieve."

Derek's chuckle carried over to me as I finished pouring my cup of coffee. "Did you want some?" I held up another mug.

"Absolutely. One of the best parts about having terminal cancer is I literally don't give a fuck what I eat or drink."

I laughed in response as I filled another mug with coffee. His comment was funny, but it hurt. A moment later, I set his coffee on the table beside the couch where he was seated. He was so thin that worry hit me hard every time I looked at him.

I sat across from him in a chair, kicking my feet up on the giant ottoman between the couch and my chair. I let my eyes arc about the space. When I discovered it was available within a month, I didn't hesitate to make an offer. Thanks to the sale of the house Derek and I had shared together a few years ago, I'd been able to pay in full without taking out a loan. That was before I started hotshot firefighting.

This house was set on a bluff near downtown Fireweed Harbor. It offered a nice view of the harbor. The backyard was fenced. That had been important because my brother's dog came with him. Charlotte, his sweet mutt, was currently out in the yard jumping around in the snow. The doggie door was convenient, so I didn't have to worry about her freezing her butt off if she needed to come in. As if Charlotte read my thoughts, she came bolting through it, stopping to shake snow all over the floor before she trotted to the couch and jumped up beside Derek. She plopped down with a satisfied sigh.

He looked over at me. "She loves it here too."

"This is a good place for a dog."

I looked from Charlotte to him, taking a slow breath before I took a gulp of coffee. The home was new, and I liked it. With clean lines, high ceilings, stainless steel appliances, and a combination of tile and light-colored wood flooring, it had an open, airy feel. It was a unique build with a tall, angled roof in the front so all the snow slid off the back. The house was nestled into a hillside to take advantage of the geothermal heat. There were plenty of windows and no stairs. This was key because walking was exhausting for Derek.

He had arrived two weeks ago. I was relieved he was here and disconcerted that I missed McKenna. I still saw her, but we had fallen into a pattern of spending every few nights together when I lived three doors down from her. We had never spoken about it again beyond our initial discussion. We had settled into a silent agreement that it couldn't be every night because that might mean something. Ever since I'd moved, we didn't even have those nights, and I missed her. A lot.

Derek wouldn't care if I wasn't here every night, but trying to explain this to him felt odd.

"You can still make a good cup of coffee." He lifted his mug, nodding before taking a healthy swallow. "That said, it's not as good as what we can get at Spill the Beans."

I chuckled. "I would agree that their coffee is better."

Derek had already settled into a routine. When I wasn't at home, he usually made his way downtown. He'd insisted on bringing his car up here so he could get around on his own. He brushed me off when I expressed any concern about whether it was a good idea for him to be driving, as weak as he was.

"That's what my handicap tag is for. I get the best parking," he'd said. "That's new for me. I'm gonna suck every benefit out of this shitty situation that I can. There are some perks to being this sick."

With Charlotte snoring softly beside Derek, we fell into a companionable silence. He startled me when he asked, "So what's going on with you and McKenna?"

He'd already met the entire Cannon family. He'd met their mother at Spill the Beans Café and become fast friends.

"What do you mean?" I countered, trying to play it cool.

Derek's brows hitched up as a sly grin stretched across his face. "Dude, I'm an observant guy. You also lived a few houses down from her, across the street from Phyllis's house. She told me you two had a thing."

I let my head fall back against the chair cushion, letting out a groan. Lifting my head, I leveled my gaze with his. "For fuck's sake. Do I seriously have to deal with gossip?"

"I don't think it's gossip if it's me. I'm your brother. I thought you told me everything." He pressed a palm to his chest in faux outrage.

I rolled my eyes. "Since when do you tell me everything?"

He snorted. Without another word, he circled his hand in the air.

I took a long swallow of coffee before lowering my mug. "We sort of have a thing. It's nothing serious."

Discomfort tightened in my chest at that description. McKenna was *so* much more than that. I knew I needed to be emotionally present for Derek, not getting confused over whether I could have something more with her—even though I had told her very clearly I never wanted anything more with her or anyone.

Derek knew me too well. His smile faded quickly as he studied me. "You like her." His tone was definitive, confident enough that I wanted to argue.

Once again, I dodged. "Of course I like her. She's nice. We're friends."

"Friends with benefits? Sure, go ahead and fool yourself."

"What do you mean?"

"When I said you like her, I meant more than just because she's nice and you're friends."

Derek was right, but I didn't want to entertain that train of thought. "Look, I'm not a good bet. My job isn't easy on any kind of relationship, and I have to—"

"Don't you dare fucking tell me you've got to focus on me, or be available for me, or some bullshit like that. You can do more than one thing at a time. You're just letting your old baggage get in the way."

"What the hell?" Annoyance spiked inside.

"You know what I mean. That whole mess that went down with Alisha. She was your first serious relationship, and you were ready to go all in. Then she guilt-tripped you about having kids and soured you on trying again."

I shifted my shoulders uncomfortably, experiencing an old but familiar pang of distrust. It wasn't like Alisha set out to hurt me, but when she admitted she hadn't been honest about wanting kids and just assumed I'd change my mind, it had carved deep grooves of cynicism for me. I was fine, fucking fine, about that now. I didn't want to admit that maybe Derek getting sick again only added to my cynicism. I didn't trust life, and I didn't want Derek to be right. "It's not that," I said quickly.

"Of course, it's that."

Looking back at my brother, I knew he spoke the truth, but it annoyed me. "Is this a side effect of cancer? You being a blunt asshole about stuff that's none of your business." My defensive tone was sharper than I intended.

It didn't rattle Derek. He cocked his head to the side, waggling his brows. "Maybe. It's me making sure you're okay before I'm gone."

His words felt like a fist punching me in the chest. The force nearly knocked the breath clean out of my lungs. "Fuck, Derek." I ran a hand through my hair with pain lacing my words.

His smile was wry, and his eyes were sad. "Dude, there's a lot of shit I wish I could do over. I have no idea if McKenna is the woman for you. But you're a good man with a good heart, and I hate to see you shutting the door to even a chance of having someone do this messy thing called life with you."

I opened my mouth to say something, but he waved his hand. "And don't give me the whole fire-fighter bullshit. Firefighters fall in love, even hotshot firefighters who travel a lot. Life is life. I'm not saying you shouldn't be alone. I'm just saying that I hate to see you box yourself out of options just because."

I took a slow breath. "Okay. But I don't think McKenna wants that. We had an actual conversation after our first night together, and well…" I shrugged.

"Well, she could be a dumbass like you," he said dryly, drawing a bark of laughter from me.

"We do agree on one important thing."

"What's that?"

"Neither one of us wants kids."

Derek studied me for a long moment. This wasn't news to him since he didn't want kids either. We used to joke about it.

"About that?"

Apprehension prickled in my awareness.

"What do you mean?"

"Uh, something happened out of the blue, and I'm going to need your help."

I drained my coffee and circled my hand in the air. The pause felt loaded and not in a good way.

"Do you remember Susan?"

"Yeah, of course, I remember her. She was your girlfriend in high school. She broke your heart when she moved away."

"She sure did," he agreed.

"Why the fuck are you looking at me like that?"

"One of her friends called me. Susan got pregnant.

Her parents made her keep it quiet when they moved away. She had the baby."

My mouth dropped open. "Oh my fucking God."

Derek nodded. "Yeah, blew my mind too."

"How long have you known this?"

"I just found out yesterday. Hannah, my daughter, wants to come up and meet me and you. Susan passed away from complications from a stroke. Her parents are also gone. I'm all my daughter has, and I didn't even know she existed until yesterday."

I stared at my brother, my eyes going wide.

"Uh, what are you planning to do?"

Chapter Twenty-Six

MCKENNA

An eagle screeched loudly nearby. I glanced over to see the bird glaring at a seagull trying to steal a fish. The eagle stalked toward the gull, who wisely flew away.

My heartbeat kicked faster. I'd seen eagles all of my life. Watching them was always exhilarating. At the sound of a splash, I glanced out toward the water to see a raft of otters drifting near the docks, a few playing in the harbor.

A blast of cold wind came off the water, and I shivered as I turned to walk back toward the docks. Just as I crested the top of the dock ramp to turn onto the sidewalk, I recognized Jack approaching. He walked beside his brother, who I'd met in passing a few times. I was trying not to think too much about it, but I missed my nights with Jack.

Remember? It was just a convenient arrangement. You don't want anything else. Things will get awkward if you try to turn it into more.

My cynical mind taunted me on the regular these days. I didn't really know what to do as Jack and Derek got closer. All I could do was play it cool. They were close enough that I felt it would be awkward to ignore them, so I waited.

I shivered slightly as they reached me. Derek shared Jack's eyes, that bright starlight blue. I forced myself to focus on Derek first. "Hi, Derek. How's Fireweed Harbor treating you?"

His eyes twinkled as a smile cracked across his thin face. "I love it."

Even though I knew he was sick, his joy was so evident it was infectious. "I've always loved it here."

"Lucky you got to grow up here," he replied.

"I am lucky."

I finally risked a glance at Jack. When his eyes met mine, my belly did a little shimmy and a twist. "Hi, Jack." I had to clear my throat after those two words.

"Good to see you, McKenna." My pulse kicked up its heels and took off in a mad dash.

Derek glanced back and forth between us, his tongue pressing into his cheek before he grinned, his eyes holding a sly gleam. "You know, you two can do your thing. Just because I'm here doesn't mean that needs to stop."

Heat flashed into my cheeks. "What?" I sputtered.

"It's time for me to leave the scene. I walk pretty slowly, so by the time I get to the coffee shop, you two can have a nice chat. Just give me a little head start," Derek quipped as he began to walk, leaning on his cane for support.

"Oh my God," I said under my breath once he was out of earshot.

I dared to look up at Jack, and his eyes glinted with humor. "He asked me about you. I tried to play it off, but apparently, Phyllis lives across the street from you." He shrugged, rolling his eyes. "I didn't mean to create gossip."

I lightly bounced the heel of my hand against my forehead and burst out laughing. "Of course! Yes, Phyllis lives across from those houses. You didn't create gossip; Phyllis did. I wonder who else she's told."

"Derek said she swore she didn't tell anyone else."

I shook my head slowly, bemused. "Small-town problems."

"My brother assures me he won't tell anyone else." He glanced ahead. Derek was just turning into the walkway that led to Spill the Beans Café. "Shall we get going? You look cold."

At my nod, we began walking. "It sounds like Derek is adjusting well. He's already got an in with Phyllis."

"That's Derek." Jack's tone was wry.

"How are you?" I asked.

Jack paused on the sidewalk, glancing down, and I waited with him. His shoulders rose as he took a deep breath. "I'm as well as could be expected." His tone was careful. "I'm really glad Derek's here even though it's hard to see him sick. I wouldn't have it any other way."

I studied him for a moment as he held my gaze steadily, not once looking away. "You're a good man, Jack Hamilton."

"I try to be. Speaking of my brother and awkward gossip, I'd love to see you."

I wasn't entirely sure how to interpret that. "You can stop by any evening. You know where I live."

When he dipped his head in acknowledgment, I added, "We might as well give Phyllis something to talk about."

He threw his head back with a laugh.

We began walking again. "So he's doing okay?"

Jack's breath puffed in the air with his response. "As okay as he can be. He's skin and bones and moves slowly, but his spirits are good. He says he's not in much pain."

"I suppose that's the best you can ask for." I felt as if my words fell short.

"I think so."

I sensed something else was on Jack's mind. "Are you sure everything's okay?" I prompted.

"Yes."

A moment later, he held the door for me at the café. The warm air was a welcome respite from the cold winter morning. It might've been April in Alaska, but spring nights and mornings were chilly. There was still snow on the mountains.

Derek had already commandeered a table and lifted his hand in a wave, calling over, "Get my order for me, would you?"

Jack cracked a grin as he nodded. When we got to the front of the line, Haven smiled at us. "Do I need to pay for my brother's order?"

Haven shook her head. "He paid for yours and McKenna's."

"He doesn't know what I'm getting," I interjected.

Haven shrugged. "He said he'll take care of it."

We ordered, and as she began prepping our coffees, she asked, "Do you want any of the Fireweed Salmon Derby tickets?"

"The what?" Jack asked, just as I replied, "Of course."

Haven handed him the informational flyer and multitasked while explaining, "Every spring, Fireweed Harbor raises money for nonprofits with a fishing tournament. Ninety percent of the money raised goes to local nonprofits, and the rest goes to cash prizes.

You don't have to fish in it, but if you don't fish, you bet on people who do fish in it."

"I'm in," Jack replied with a chuckle.

We were seated at the table a few minutes later, and Derek was all about the salmon derby. "If I win one of the cash prizes, I'll have a few hundred bucks to blow before I die. If I die, then that's more money for you and Hannah."

Jack took a gulp of his coffee, shifting in his seat. The gap in the conversation felt loaded, and Derek's bluntness was something to behold.

"Have you told McKenna about Hannah?" Derek pressed.

"Oh, for fuck's sake, Derek. I haven't had time to fill her in on all of that," Jack muttered.

I looked back and forth between them. "If it's none of my business, nobody needs to tell me anything."

Derek nodded vigorously as he finished chewing a bite of his bagel, which was generously slathered in smoked salmon cream cheese. After he finished his bite, he took a swallow of coffee. "I didn't know I had a daughter until a few days ago." My eyes must've gone wide because he nodded vigorously. "No shit. It's crazy. We're her only family. Her mom died. She has no grandparents, and her mom was an only child. Her grandparents were kind of controlling and shitty, so she doesn't know any extended family on that side." Derek appeared wildly calm about this massive piece of news.

I looked at Jack, who shrugged. I glanced back toward Derek who took another bite of his bagel.

"How do you feel about that?" I finally asked, unsure where the hell else to start.

Derek cocked his head to the side. "Her mom

totally broke my heart. We were in love in high school, and I thought she dumped me. What I didn't know was her parents moved out of town because she got pregnant. This was before cell phones were all that common, so once she moved, I didn't know how to reach her, and her parents didn't want her calling me." He paused, shaking his head. "Damn, they were fucking assholes. "Anyway, my daughter is seventeen years old now. I told her that she can come stay with us. Jack is saying really a whole lot of nothing about it, so I'm hoping you'll get him to talk about it."

I looked from Jack to Derek and back again. "Um, you seem very calm about this."

Derek let out a sigh. "I gave myself twenty-four hours to panic, and I freaked right the fuck out. I was pissed off too. I can't believe what happened. But there's literally nothing I can do to change the past. I'm not gonna leave my daughter alone in the world. I'm reconsidering chemo."

"You didn't mention that." Jack's tone was sharp.

Derek waved in Jack's direction. "Hey, the guy finally speaks. Yeah. I'll be fucking miserable, but I have a daughter. If I can somehow beat the odds and get better, I'll fucking do it. If I get better, you can help me find a place, and we'll stay here."

Jack just stared at Derek. I wasn't thinking when I reached over and placed my palm on his thigh under the table. I could sense the intensity of his emotions. His jaw was tight with a muscle clenching in his cheek. He tore off a bite of his bagel, chewing vigorously before he set it down and reached for his coffee. He slid his other hand under the table, lacing his fingers with mine and squeezing.

"One way or another, it'll be okay." I said the only thing that seemed to make sense no matter how small or inadequate it felt. "If you want some advice on a child showing up out of the blue, you can talk to anyone in my family. Our oldest brother Jake died. Maybe you've heard that because this town is kind of gossipy. He had a son that none of us knew about. It was kind of a shock. It's weird to have someone show up like that."

Derek angled his head to the side before taking a long swallow of coffee. He straightened in his chair, his gaze very serious as he looked at me. "I know I might sound a little flippant, but getting a potentially terminal illness can do that to you. The whole thing *is* weird. I think I might be freaking right the fuck out still, except I'm just kind of running straight at it. I got Hannah a plane ticket, and she'll be here tomorrow. Jack says it's okay."

I squeezed Jack's hand. "As if it would be anything other than okay. I'm just absorbing a lot right now. You might try not to die, and you have a daughter," Jack said so earnestly my heart twisted for him. "I'll be there for her if you're not here, but now I want you to fucking fight." His voice cracked on the last word.

Derek held his gaze steadily. "I'm gonna fucking fight."

"Should we go back to Seattle?" Jack asked suddenly.

I was scrambling to keep up with the turns in this conversation and lost the thread here.

Derek knew exactly what Jack was talking about and shook his head swiftly. "You did the legwork for me already. The treatment center in Juneau has one of the top surgeons from the chemo program in Seattle. He travels between Juneau and Seattle. I need to be here."

"I'll go with you if you need me," Jack offered quickly.

Derek shook his head again. "Being with you is important, but it's also this place. I love Alaska. I always have. Maybe that doesn't make sense, but it doesn't matter. I need to be right here."

Emotion rushed through me. I looked around the café a moment later to realize everything was just carrying on around us. A monumental conversation was happening, and life simply moved along.

After several moments of quiet, Derek looked at me. "I appreciate your feedback on a child showing up out of the blue. I'd heard about that. You guys are kind of like the *hot* family in town." He waggled his brows, the lightness of his tone much needed at that moment.

I rolled my eyes as Jack chuckled. He kept his fingers laced with mine and ate his bagel with one hand, sipping his coffee between bites.

A short while later, I stood, glancing back and forth between them. "All right, guys, I have to go to work. Stay out of trouble today."

Derek winked at me. "You take Jack tonight, please."

My cheeks were hot as I narrowed my eyes at Derek while Jack grinned at us. I was turning away when he caught my hand and squeezed. "I'll see you tonight."

My entire body was on fire as I walked out. It felt as if sparks of joy danced inside me.

Now what?

Chapter Twenty-Seven

JACK

That evening, anticipation was a rolling crescendo in my body when I stood in front of McKenna's door. I took a breath and knocked quickly.

The moment she opened the door, the electricity sizzled between us. I took a step inside when she stepped back, kicking the door shut with my boot while I cupped her cheeks and kissed her.

When we broke apart, she looked up at me. "Wow," she breathed.

I didn't even try to hide my smile or play it cool. "It's been a long few weeks."

Everything that followed was a blur. We tugged at each other's clothes while kissing. Our teeth banged, and our foreheads collided. At that point, McKenna yelped, "Ouch!"

I lifted my head. "Are you okay?"

She stood in front of me, naked save for a pair of fuzzy hot-pink socks.

Her eyes were bright as she nodded. "Are you okay?"

I was naked too, and I didn't even have my socks on. "More than okay."

She started to lean down and take one of her socks off. "Oh no, don't take those off," I said.

She peered up at me. "Why not?"

"Because you're adorable in hot pink socks."

She giggled when I kissed her again and lifted her in my arms.

For the first time in weeks, I carried her into her bedroom and stretched her out on the bed. I didn't mean for it to feel this way, but the atmosphere was intense and intimate. We couldn't get enough of each other. We were in a hurry the first time. When I brought my weight down over her and sank inside her, I brushed her tangled hair away from her forehead, whispering, "Look at me, sweetheart."

When her eyes lifted and I rocked my hips back to fill her again, I couldn't look away. I watched until I felt the torch song of her body rising to a crescendo. I followed her over the edge, and we cried out together.

Lounging in bed a little while later, I couldn't stop touching her. I wanted her soft weight against me, the feel of her skin, sliding my fingers through her hair and stealing every touch I could.

I remembered her words earlier—that one way or another, it would be okay. I was starting to wonder if I was falling for her.

With all my worries about my brother, hope was busy shooting flares into the sky for him. With his daughter coming in the thick of this, I wasn't afraid, but it was a lot to face.

Amidst all that, McKenna felt like my sanctuary, the calm center of the storm swirling around me. I couldn't talk myself out of my feelings. I couldn't talk myself out of needing her more than just physically.

I might have to pay a price, but it was a price I was more than willing to pay.

Chapter Twenty-Eight

MCKENNA

The following morning

After a steaming shower with Jack, I went to the kitchen to start a pot of coffee for us. The coffee was better at Spill the Beans Café, but I wasn't ready to face the world yet. I felt too raw, physically and emotionally.

Jack was in my bedroom, making a few calls. He was arranging flights to the medical center for his brother and confirming the travel schedule for his niece.

I savored this time with him and needed a few minutes to gather myself. Last night had been beyond intense. We'd reached for each other more than once in the darkness. The last time we had made sleepy love, I'd woken in the dark with him curled behind me. I was already aroused and felt him come awake. He'd dusted a kiss on my neck, asking, "Are you awake?"

My answer had been to rock my hips back on his

velvety hard arousal nestled against my bottom. A moment later, he filled me from behind and fucked me, lazily and sensually, teasing me to a shuddering climax with his fingers.

I'd never been so physically sated in my entire life. Now, I feared I was in way too deep. I was barely treading water in the depths of my feelings.

I puttered around the kitchen like I usually did in the mornings. All of a sudden, he was right behind me, saying, "Coffee smells good."

I nearly jumped out of my skin. I spun around, my eyes wide and my heart pounding in a panicked beat. He looked as surprised as I felt and studied me for a moment.

"I didn't mean to startle you," he finally said, his tone calm and level while he looked at me like I was some kind of feral animal. "It seems like I've said that too many times with you."

"I forgot you were here," I explained in a rush.

Jack's curious eyes coasted over my face, but he nodded without adding anything. I wanted to smooth things over and started babbling about coffee and whether he wanted anything to eat.

A few minutes passed, and we were sitting at the counter. After he took a swallow of coffee, he asked, "Has anyone hurt you?"

My jaw went slack as I stared at him. Literally nobody had ever asked me about my wildly unmeasured startle reflex, not even my family. I wanted to lie but didn't, yet I only shared part of the truth.

I took a long swallow of coffee to fortify myself. "If you haven't heard from the rumors in town, you will eventually. Our dad died when I was little. After he died, my grandparents helped a lot. Our grandfather was abusive, mostly verbally, but he used to get physical with Rhys and Jake." I took a quick breath, ignoring the sickening feeling I felt whenever I said Jake's name. "He never hit me, but he yelled."

Jack stared at me for a long moment. "I'm really sorry."

"It's okay." I shrugged. "It's life, I guess. Everybody's got something."

"I guess so. You don't need to apologize for startling easy. Now that I know, I can be careful not to startle you. I can maybe just say something sooner when you don't see me."

A rush of emotion crested inside. "You don't have to do that," I said, thinking that seemed ridiculous to expect.

He held my gaze. "McKenna, I want to."

I didn't even know what to do with that.

———

A few weeks later

Time was quickening, but that was how it always felt in spring. I'd met Derek's daughter. Hannah was friendly and seemed understandably emotionally shell-shocked about her situation. Meanwhile, Jack stopped by every third or fourth night to stay with me.

I wrestled with myself because I was in love with him, and I knew it. I wanted all sorts of things I'd never sought before. Meanwhile, I kept my feelings quiet. Jack was tied up with his brother's treatment and helping his niece adjust.

I was an expert at this. I knew how to keep my shit together, no matter what was going on around me. Given our messy family, I'd had to learn to do that.

It was locals' night at Fireweed Winery, and Jack had brought Derek and his niece along. My mom sat with Derek and Hannah while Jack chatted with Griffin about something. Wyatt appeared beside me where I stood nearby.

"So you're in love," he said matter-of-factly.

"What?!" I turned to face him fully.

"Sis, I'm pretty sure you are. What are you gonna do about it?"

"Nothing! We're not serious," I insisted.

Wyatt studied me for a long minute. "Why not? You deserve love."

It felt as if Wyatt had kicked open a door I kept shut, locked, and bolted for good measure. I didn't like to think about love. Maybe I didn't think I deserved it.

This was an inconvenient place for any kind of serious conversation, but I couldn't walk away. "Why do you say that?" I finally asked.

I'd always been closer to Wyatt than my other brothers. He and Griffin were the closest in age to me. "Because I get it. I'm no expert, but our family was kind of fucked up. Or the grown-ups were. Everybody except Mom."

"And Dad," I chimed in.

Wyatt shrugged, almost dismissive about that. "We all had to live with our grandfather, and you had to live with Jake. You still have to live with listening to everybody else talk about Jake like he was fucking perfect. After what he went through, I get it. But he wasn't because he took his own shit out on you. Does it mean you deserved it? I imagine maybe you wonder that sometimes. None of us deserved any of it."

I stared at my brother, almost stunned at the clarity of his observation.

"Thank you," I finally said.

"For what?"

"For letting me know you saw what happened with Jake. I've always just gotten quiet when everybody talks about him. I still miss him, but..." I shrugged, unsure how to explain the mixed emotions I experienced when talking about my oldest brother. Jake wasn't all bad, but it was hard to forget being the target of his misplaced anger.

Wyatt stepped closer, sliding his arm around my shoulders. It felt as if he imparted some of his strength to me.

I looked up at him as he stepped back. "Do you think it's worth saying something to the rest of the family?" I asked softly.

Wyatt glanced around. Our siblings were scattered around the room while our mother talked with Derek and his daughter. "That's up to you. I'll have your back. But if you plan to say anything to anybody, maybe start with Mom."

I took a slow breath. "I'll think about it."

Just then, Blake appeared, cuffing Wyatt lightly on the shoulder. "All right, dude. You start next month. Are you ready?"

Wyatt held my gaze for another few seconds, dipping his chin in acknowledgment before he turned toward Blake and nodded firmly. "Absolutely."

Blake pulled him into a back-slapping hug. Blake was so happy Wyatt and Griffin were moving back to Fireweed Harbor. We all were.

"I'm stoked! You've got free rein to run the show in the brewery. McKenna handles marketing, so keep her in the loop for anything new."

Wyatt chuckled just as Griffin made his way over, and the conversation moved on.

Later that night, Jack came over. It was another night when I felt cleaved wide open. I was awake in bed beside Jack, listening to the even rhythm of his breath when I recalled Wyatt's observations. He thought I was in love with Jack and that I deserved love. What the hell was I supposed to do with that?

Chapter Twenty-Nine

JACK

"Well?" Derek prompted.

I slid my gaze to my brother. "Well, what?"

"How are you?"

I glanced around our kitchen. Derek was usually up first and always made a pot of coffee. We'd fallen into a pattern of lounging in the kitchen while the sun rose. Charlotte liked to go outside if it was sunny or snooze beside the table if it wasn't.

Hannah was settling in and had enrolled in school two weeks prior. Our parents were planning to come up for a weekend visit to meet her. She had taken an after-school job at the winery kitchen as a prep cook. Fiona, Blake's wife, drove by our place every day, so she'd started taking her to school. Hannah had left a few minutes earlier.

"We've been up together for an hour. I'm fine. Why are you asking me this now?"

"Because you don't seem fucking fine," my brother retorted.

I bought myself a little time by walking over to

pour the rest of the coffee into my mug. I rinsed the coffee pot out and called over my shoulder, "Should I make another pot of coffee?"

"Nah."

I *was* fine, in the sense of being fine enough to carry on with the day-to-day activities of life and work. But I was also not particularly fine. With Derek starting chemo again, I was terrified it wouldn't work. I didn't even know how to process that. When he'd decided not to try treatment again, I'd had to wrestle my hope for his recovery into submission. Now, I was afraid to hope too much.

I also struggled with Hannah's sudden appearance in our life. It wasn't a struggle at all to have her in the house. She was polite and quiet. She went out of her way to make it seem like she wasn't even here.

And *that* worried me. I didn't want her to think she was an inconvenience and a burden to us because she wasn't. At all. But my brother had a daughter, and neither one of us knew her until very recently. Now, she was here, and Derek, me, our parents and cluster of relatives were all she had to call family. It was a lot to take in.

I took a swallow of coffee, the rich flavor reminding me that our coffee didn't quite measure up to what we could get at Spill the Beans Café. I remembered yesterday morning, waking up curled around McKenna. I hadn't wanted to get out of bed. I loved being with her, and I was pretty sure I'd gone and fallen in love with her. Which was fucking stupid.

It would be an understatement to say I had too much going on. I didn't have the emotional bandwidth for love.

I sat down across from my brother and leveled my gaze with his. "I think I fucked up with McKenna."

"Oh?"

Although my brother could be sarcastic, he never was in a clutch moment. His gaze was steady and patient.

I took another swallow of coffee, running my hand through my hair after I set my mug on the table. "I just don't have time."

Derek cocked his head to the side, one brow rising sharply in question. "You seem to be making time every few nights."

I rolled my eyes. "I'm not a good bet, you know that. My job takes me away for weeks and sometimes months at a time."

"And what? Are you going to say you're busy dealing with me and my cancer treatment?"

"Derek, there's no way I wouldn't help. That's not an option. I love you."

Derek let out a sharp sigh. "That's not what I meant. I get it because it would be the same for me. It's clear you and McKenna love each other."

I opened my mouth to question him, but he dismissed me with a quick wave. "Staring the potential for death in its face kinda makes some things very obvious. You love her. That matters. The details don't."

"What if you don't make it?" My eyes stung with tears, and my heart ached. That was the thing about fucking cancer. When someone you loved had it, you had to prepare for the worst, but it was impossible not to hope things worked out. Cancer was a fucking asshole.

Derek shrugged, acting way too relaxed, in my opinion. "I may not, but I'm going to fight like hell. I want to be there for Hannah."

I listened to my brother's lecture about love and so

on while I quietly reminded myself that I couldn't make space for someone else to matter too much until I knew Derek would survive.

Chapter Thirty

MCKENNA

I turned off my car in front of my mother's house and took a slow breath. I listened to the soft ticking sound as the engine cooled. Before I could think too long about it, I climbed out quickly, tucking my keys in my jacket pocket, and jogged to the door.

My mother always insisted we didn't have to knock, but it felt strange to walk in unannounced. I usually knocked and called out my name as I walked in.

"In the kitchen!" my mother answered in return.

On the heels of another deep breath, I walked into the kitchen. She sat at the counter, flipping through a magazine, and smiled at me. "Coffee? Or tea?"

My throat felt dry, but I knew I couldn't drink anything, so I shook my head. I sat across from her at the island, hooking my feet around the legs of the stool.

"How are you?" she asked.

"Jake used to hit me." My words came out in a rush and a little louder than I intended.

My mother's face went blank, and her hands stilled. "What do you mean?"

My heart pounded an unsteady beat, and I felt a little sick. I'd been working on getting up my nerve to just tell her about Jake for what felt like forever. I'd always wanted to tell her, but until Wyatt had told me he knew, I had accepted it would be my secret. Jake represented too many important things for the family, especially our mother.

"Just that. Jake used to bully me and hit me."

"Are you sure?" my mother pressed.

Anger rose in a fiery rush, and I didn't even know where that came from.

"Of course I'm sure, Mom. I don't know what you know about abuse and the kind of abuse Jake experienced, but it's not shocking for someone to lash out and treat others the way they were treated. Granddad was awful to all of us. He used to hit Jake, and then he raped him. You know this. Why is it so crazy to think Jake might lash out at someone? My therapist —"

My mother's eyes narrowed. "Did your therapist convince you of this? Is that what happened?" I was so taken aback by her reaction that I almost got up and left. I forced myself to stay and see this through.

"No, Mom. I always remembered this. Jake used to enjoy scaring the shit out of me from behind. He would shove me and hit me. I loved him too. It wasn't always bad, but I'm trying to be honest with you. We have too many secrets in our family."

My mother's nostrils flared. "Okay. Why are you telling me this now?"

"Because I'm tired of hiding it. I know you're still going to be sad, and you're going to miss Jake, but it's exhausting to pretend he was some kind of saint. He wasn't."

"I don't think your brother was a saint."

"Well, you act like he was, Mom!" I swallowed through the tight ball of pain in my throat. I felt hot all over. "I'm here, and I'm alive. You don't do Jake's memory any favors by pretending he was perfect."

"Did he hurt your brothers?"

I shrugged because I didn't actually know. I sensed something might have happened with Wyatt, but I honestly wasn't sure. "If you don't believe me, ask Wyatt. He saw Jake hit me. More than once."

My mother stayed quiet. I didn't know how to read her expression.

"Well?" I pressed.

"Honey, this is a shock to me. I'm sorry if I'm not reacting the way you expected."

That was all I could take. I stood and walked swiftly out of the house. I ignored my mother calling my name as she followed me to the front door.

Minutes later, I was driving and swiping away the hot tears rolling down my cheeks. I was supposed to return to the office but didn't want to. I couldn't face anyone right now. Instead, I parked my car at my house and walked to the docks. I went down a side trail leading to the beach and sat on one of my favorite rocks. It had this little dip in it, perfect for sitting.

My mother's words echoed in my thoughts. I didn't know what I had expected from her, but I wanted her to believe me.

My tears dried as I concluded that it didn't really matter. All this time, I kept quiet, and nothing was really different now that I'd told the truth. If anything, I felt worse.

I wanted comfort, and the first person who came to mind was Jack. That was a problem. I could sense him pulling back the last few times I'd seen him. The next time he texted or called about coming over, I resolved I would tell him maybe it wasn't a good idea.

———

"I told Mom."

Wyatt had stopped by my office because he was filling out the official paperwork with HR now that he was working for us again.

His eyes widened. He closed the door behind him and walked across my office to sit in front of my desk. "You did?"

I felt numb about the whole thing. "I did. I'm not sure she believed me. She asked me if I was sure. I hope it's okay that I told her you'd seen Jake hit me."

Wyatt's expression was hard to read as he studied me. "It's fine. Do you want to talk to anybody else about it?"

I looked down at my desk, idly tracing along the grain of the wood. "I don't know."

"Griffin knows, and he believes you."

"I know. You mentioned that before."

Wyatt's gaze remained inscrutable as he nodded. "Do you mind if I mention it to Rhys? I just don't want you to feel alone. It's no secret that Jake was troubled. I mean, fuck, he drank himself to death in college. If you ask me not to say anything to anyone else, I won't."

I pondered my other siblings knowing and realized I didn't really care anymore. "You can tell Rhys. Or anyone else. It's fine."

There was another knock on my door, and Blake leaned inside. He flashed a quick grin in Wyatt's direction. "Are you all lined up?"

"Sure thing. I'll be at the brewery tomorrow."

"Good deal. Catch you later. Will you both be at locals' night?"

Blake left after we nodded. I was relieved he didn't linger because I wasn't ready to talk more about it.

A few minutes later, Wyatt got ready to leave, and I stood to walk him to the door. "Bring it in," he said, holding his arms out. He gave me a big hug. I didn't realize how much I needed that hug. When he stepped back, he studied me. "I'm proud of you."

"You are?"

"You've got more courage than I do. Telling the truth, especially when people don't want to hear it, takes a lot."

That evening, I was about to gather my jacket and purse to walk from our main offices across the street to the winery when there was a knock on my office door.

"Come in!" I called, curious as to who it would be. Once our official office hours ended, the building tended to be fairly quiet unless someone worked late.

My mother peered inside the door, her gaze hesitant when she saw me. "Is it okay if I come in?"

"Of course." My fingers curled tightly around my purse, and I held it in front of me, almost like a shield.

My mother closed the door behind her with a decisive click. She studied me for a moment. "I owe you an apology," she finally said.

"You do?"

"I do. I believe you about Jake. I wasn't supportive of you when you told me, and I'm sorry."

I blinked quickly. "Did you talk to Wyatt?"

She shook her head sharply. "I didn't need to talk to Wyatt to choose to believe you. I have a lot of guilt about how things went after your father died. I don't know how to fix everything. I knew Jake had a temper.

It isn't surprising that he hit you. I hope that's all it was."

The following pause was long. I knew she was asking me to fill this gap in information. Jake had also been sexually abused by our grandfather, a detail none of us had known until years after his death.

"No. Nothing like that ever happened, Mom. Jake was a bully to me. He wasn't always, and I loved him too. I promise. Loving him, in a way, kind of made it worse. I'm not sure why I decided to say something after all this time. I think I was just tired of keeping it a secret."

She took a few steps closer and reached out, placing a hand on my shoulder. Her touch was warm and reassuring. "I'm sorry it happened. I'm sorry I didn't protect you." She blinked, her eyes shining with tears. "I'm sorry I didn't protect all of you."

"Grandfather was as bad to you as he was to the rest of us," I pointed out. I remembered him yelling at her too.

Her mouth twisted to the side as bitterness flashed in her gaze. "He yelled at me, but he never laid a hand on me. I feel like I failed all of you."

"It's okay, Mom."

She looked into my eyes as her hand fell away from my shoulder. "I hope it is. I'm still going to miss Jake. I'm sad about what happened to him. I'm sad about what happened to you, and I'm sad for all of us."

We ended up walking together over to locals' night, and after a difficult few days, I felt a little lighter.

I was also feeling tender and emotionally raw. When Jack asked, "Can I stop by tonight?" I shook my head.

Chapter Thirty-One

JACK

As I watched McKenna slip out the side door, I wanted to follow her. I wanted to ask her why I couldn't stop by tonight.

The conversation carried on around me. Hannah's voice snapped through my distraction. "Is that McKenna?" My niece stood beside my brother, who was busy talking with Rhys.

"Haven't you met McKenna?" I asked.

I knew Hannah had met her because we'd run into McKenna one morning at the coffee shop. She nodded. "She's the one you like."

My niece said this as if she was reciting a fact, like the color of the sky being blue.

I opened my mouth to refute that point but stopped when I realized I was about to debate this with my seventeen-year-old niece. Hannah's smile was sly. "McKenna's a very nice person. Of course I like her," I replied blandly.

"Nice like me," Griffin quipped when he appeared by my shoulder.

Griffin was joining my hotshot crew, so we'd started to get to know each other.

I chuckled. "Yeah, nice like you."

"Who's nice? I don't even know who you're talking about."

I almost groaned. Fuck my life. I did not need my niece deciding to stir the pot and give away anything about my feelings for McKenna. She had already asked me more than once where I spent the night when I wasn't at the house.

"Your whole family is nice," Hannah said, smoothly rescuing me from a potentially awkward moment. "You're the firefighter, right?"

"Sure am," Griffin replied. "Like your uncle here." He cuffed me lightly on the shoulder.

"Why don't you work for your family's corporation?" she asked.

Griffin pondered that before shrugging. "I probably will someday. I can't be a hotshot firefighter forever."

When Hannah looked my way again, her brow was furrowed with worry. My heart twisted a little inside. She was worried about her dad, *and* she'd already lost her mom. I didn't need her to worry about me.

"Don't you even worry about me," I said quickly.

"I'm allowed to worry about you," she said pointedly.

Griffin glanced back and forth between us. "I'll make sure he doesn't do anything stupid when we're out in the field this summer."

A little while later, when I began walking home, I contemplated that Hannah had experienced more than enough loss in her life. She needed to know I would be there, no matter what.

I told myself I was walking because I wanted the

fresh air and wasn't going to check in with McKenna. I kept hoping I would run into her anyway. Although, I knew logically she had to already be home now.

When I passed the harbor and looked toward the docks to see her standing there, my feet aimed straight for her.

As I approached, I called her name. I saw her physically jolt a little before she turned.

"Hey," I said quickly.

"Hi." Her smile was polite, and her eyes guarded.

"Is everything okay?" I asked. I didn't quite know how to read her expression, but she looked out of sorts.

When a gust of air blew off the water, and she curled her shoulders forward, I wanted to hold her. I wanted to keep her warm and protect her.

She didn't answer my question. "I think maybe we should just be friends, *just* friends," she said, emphasizing just.

For a moment, I wanted to argue about it, tell her we didn't need to do that and tell her I loved her.

Instead, I thought about Derek. I thought about the list of appointments pinned to our refrigerator. I thought about Hannah, whose life had been shaken and stirred, and I told myself it was all for the best.

"Okay. So I'll see you around then?"

McKenna blinked and glanced away. When she looked back up at me, it was as if she had closed the shades on her expressive eyes.

"Sure."

We stood there for a long moment before I forced myself to walk away. "Have a good night."

Chapter Thirty-Two

MCKENNA

My oldest brother Rhys sat across from me at his desk. Rhys was kind of intense, and he looked serious at the moment. He steepled his fingers under his chin before dipping his head in acknowledgment. "Wyatt told me."

"Huh?"

He leaned back in his chair, letting his hands fall. "He said he told you he was going to tell me." My brother looked concerned, worried even.

"He did. Sorry, I'm just catching up."

"I'm sorry about what happened."

"Not your fault," I said quickly, wanting to smooth it over and make everything okay.

The urge to smooth problems away, to make tension disappear was something that came with the territory of experiencing any kind of abuse.

"I know it's not my fault," Rhys replied. "Maybe I never saw Jake hit you, but I knew he had a temper. He never laid a hand on me. I hope it's okay that I asked Adam, Blake, and Kenan if he ever hit them."

"Not Griffin?" I asked.

"Wyatt said Griffin already told him Jake never hit him."

"Oh."

"I wish you had told me sooner."

I blinked, my eyes stinging. "Maybe I should've said something sooner, but I didn't know how to tell anyone."

"Does it bother you that Haven and I named little Jake after him?"

I shook my head quickly. "No!" Even though I had bad memories of Jake, they weren't attached to his name. It was more the secret of it. "I guess I just got tired of keeping it hidden from everybody."

"Do you want to talk about it?" Rhys pressed.

I could tell he was concerned and wanted to fix this somehow. It was really sweet for him to try to help, to be there.

"I appreciate that. I still see my therapist sometimes."

"I just want you to know if you want to talk about it, I'm here for you," Rhys insisted.

"I love that that's important to you. But really—" I swallowed. "I just didn't want to keep it a secret anymore. There's a lot of good in our family too."

Rhys held my gaze. "Maybe we should do family therapy."

I burst out laughing. "That would be a shit show. There are seven of us and Mom. Honestly, I don't think we need that. We all love each other. Maybe all we need to do is cut it out with keeping secrets."

Rhys pressed his lips together as he nodded slowly. "Maybe."

There was a knock on Rhys's office door. "Yes?" Rhys called.

Kenan came in, glancing at us. "Group hug?" he asked, reading the room quickly.

We laughed together. I didn't need to process this with my siblings, but having the truth out there was a relief. As much as I wanted to undo what happened, to erase the fact that Jake had bullied me and been physically abusive at times, I couldn't. At least I didn't have to keep it secret anymore.

After we did, in fact, have a group hug, Kenan kept his arm around my shoulders. He ruffled my hair with one hand, the way he did when I was a little girl. "You good?"

I lifted my chin as I nodded. None of this was perfect, and it was a little messy, but I wasn't alone.

Chapter Thirty-Three

MCKENNA

That afternoon, I walked to the harbor. Even though I'd grown up in Alaska, I still marveled at the sense of time stretching rapidly as the days got longer.

My heart twisted a little in my chest when I thought of Jack. I thought of him far too much. I was trying *really* hard not to miss him. I'd been busy giving myself plenty of pep talks about how I had never intended to fall in love, and this was all for the best.

As I walked down the street, I impulsively decided to stop by Spill the Beans Café. As bad luck would have it, Cory and Heather were in there. As much as I wanted to turn around and walk out, I didn't. I reminded myself that he was just a jerk who tried to capitalize on other people's pain. It stung to feel used like that.

"Hey," a voice said by my elbow.

I glanced over to see Tessa. "Hey! How is your training going?" I was relieved to have someone to talk to.

She smiled brightly. "I love it."

Tessa had taken a new job as a local weather reporter. "That's awesome!"

She waggled her brows. "It actually is! I feel so silly to be so excited."

"Don't. You have a job you love. You've been scrambling to figure things out since the divorce, and this will make it work."

"I just hope it goes well."

Tessa's formerly sunny and light personality had dimmed far too much during her marriage. I still wanted to kick her ex's ass when I saw him around town, but I focused on her positive changes instead.

"You're going to be amazing! I know this for a fact."

"You're just saying that because you're my friend," she said as we got to the front of the line.

It was crowded here this afternoon, and Hazel and Phyllis worked rapidly to make orders. A few minutes later, we sat down with our coffees.

"I'm really glad things are turning around for you," I commented.

"Since I finally walked away from the biggest mistake of my life?" Tessa mused, her tone resigned.

"Tessa, we all fuck up." I thumbed in the direction of Cory.

Tessa didn't even spare him a glance. "Oh, he's just an ass. That podcast was a dick move. And you dated him in high school, like forever ago. Who cares? We all get a pass on our poor judgment in dating when we're young."

"You should listen to your own advice," I countered with a warm smile.

She shrugged. "I don't want to dwell on me. Speaking of..." She nudged her head toward Cory. He and Heather broke up, and he's moving out of town."

If I'd been wondering if Cory could still get to me, I knew then he couldn't. My internal reaction was nothing, so I shrugged. "Moving is a pain in the ass," I offered.

Tessa's lips quirked. "Seriously. Anyway, how are you and Jack?"

"We're not."

"What do you mean?"

"We were never really a couple. I don't ever want to have a family, and being single is better. Right?"

Tessa stared at me for a long moment. "Maybe. I really thought he liked you. Like not sort of, but *really*."

I shrugged. "But it doesn't really matter. I don't want to get serious with anyone, so it's for the best."

The bell chimed on the door, and out of reflex, I glanced over. My heart gave a resounding kick against my ribs when Jack came walking in with Derek and Hannah.

When he happened to glance my way and our eyes met from across the café, my hormones cheered, and heat spun in fiery pinwheels through me. Tessa cleared her throat, and I dragged my eyes away. My cheeks were burning up.

"Good thing it's over," she said dryly.

"Oh my God," I muttered before taking a gulp of coffee.

Her grin was sly.

Hannah walked across the café. For a minute, I thought she was coming over to us, but she stopped at the empty table right beside us. When she glanced toward us, she smiled. "Oh, hi, McKenna."

"Hi, Hannah. This is Tessa." I quickly introduced them.

Hannah thought that Tessa training to be a

weather person was "the freaking most awesome thing ever" and asked Tessa tons of questions about it.

I steeled myself to deal with Jack when he and his brother approached the table beside us. Derek greeted us and reported he'd won a small cash prize from the salmon derby. "I'll be buying random coffees for people with it," he announced with a grin.

Conversation rumbled around us, and Jack's look was inscrutable when he met my gaze.

It doesn't matter, I reminded myself. *You got what you wanted. Just friends with benefits. You knew it wasn't going to be more.*

But what if it could?

I was relieved to have Tessa there. She kept the conversation rolling, with her, Derek, and Hannah doing most of the talking. I practically guzzled my coffee and got up to leave, not paying much attention to the conversation.

Tessa caught my eye. "Hannah was wondering about beach hikes. I don't know the beaches as well as you do. I'm trying to remember how to get to that old trail we used to take in high school. Do you know?"

"I can tell you how to get there."

"That would be awesome!" Hannah glanced from Derek to Jack. "Can I go?"

"Of course," Derek said. "I sure as hell can't keep up with you, though. I'd prefer it if you went with someone. There might be moose there."

It was a great spot for eagle viewing, and there most certainly could be moose around. Moose were almost always around in this part of Alaska.

When I looked toward Hannah and saw the hopefulness in her eyes, I decided to just roll with it. A few minutes later, we were walking down the sidewalk.

"I think Jack, I mean Uncle Jack, likes you," she announced.

I glanced her way. "Uh, well..." I hedged.

She smiled shyly. "I know you barely know me, but he totally has a thing for you. I'm just saying."

Hope shot up flares in my heart, but I ignored it. I didn't trust myself. Maybe Jack did like me, but that was chemistry. I knew he didn't want to suddenly change his life and have a serious relationship.

I shrugged. "Okay."

When I didn't say anything else, she shifted gears, saying, "It's still weird to call him uncle."

"I can imagine. How are you doing? This is a big change for you," I offered.

Hannah glanced at me quickly before looking away as we continued walking. "It's okay. I'm okay. It's been a weird year. My mom died, and Derek, I mean Dad, is all I have. And he's sick." Her voice cracked on the last word.

When I looked her way, her eyes were on the trees ahead. "I bet that's hard. I bet this whole thing is hard."

"It is." She lifted her chin, but she didn't look my way.

I wanted to give her the space she so obviously needed, so I didn't add anything. We fell into quiet as we walked. A few moments later, I gestured to the side. "Down here."

Hannah followed me down to the harbor. I showed her the gravel path that led to the beach away from the docks. "I used to hike all the time when I was younger," I explained as we walked.

"Tessa said this is a good spot to see the sea lions," Hannah said.

"It is. They often rest on some rocks in the water."

We picked our way over a rocky section of the trail. "This isn't an official trail. When the tide comes in, the water closes it off for a few hours."

I could see the tide was rolling in, but I guessed we had a few hours.

"That's kind of cool," Hannah said after a moment.

"That's why I've always liked this trail. The view is incredible, and it's never a busy spot."

We traveled in silence for a little while and crossed over the area the tide would eventually cover when it came in. Even though I hadn't planned on this for today, I enjoyed the hike and needed the fresh air and scenery to break me out of my funk. With the trail following the shoreline, it offered a gorgeous view.

"Almost there," I said when I recognized the landmark on the trail that would lead us to the area with some rocky clusters in the water.

As soon as we came around the corner, nature gave us a show. Some seals lounged in the sunshine on one big rock, with sea lions farther ahead on another boulder in the water.

Hannah bounced on her toes. "Oh wow," she breathed. "They're amazing." She looked from the seals to the sea lions. "Wow, sea lions are seriously big."

I chuckled. "They are."

"Are they here often?"

As we stood there, a curious seal occasionally poked its head out of the water near the shoreline as if checking on us.

"Pretty often. It's a good sunny spot, so I assume they like it." I glanced at my watch. "We should probably go soon. We need to make sure we're back well before the tide comes in too far."

Hannah took a few photos with her phone camera

before we began walking back. We rounded a corner in the trail along a rocky section. Hannah took a step and slipped. In a matter of seconds, she had fallen halfway down the gravelly bluff.

She let out a startled and pained cry.

"Are you okay?" I called down.

"I think so. I hurt my ankle. Just give me a minute," she called up.

A moment later, she began to climb up before letting out a yelp. "McKenna?"

"Yeah?"

"Something's wrong with my ankle. I think it's broken."

I could hear the tears in her voice. I knew I could get to her. Except the tide would be coming in some-time soon. If she couldn't walk, I didn't know how I was going to get her off the cliff with a broken ankle. I slipped my phone out of my pocket and swore when I saw the single bar for reception.

"Shit," I muttered.

"Hannah, you stay right where you are," I called down in my most comforting voice.

I crossed my fingers and prayed as I called. The call dropped as soon as I heard one ring. I quickly texted my brothers. I figured Rhys would respond first because he tended to monitor his phone closely.

Hannah is with me. I took her down to see the sea lions. Check with Tessa about it. It's the trail near the harbor through the tall grass. Hannah thinks she broke her ankle. I'm not sure I can get her all the way back by myself.

After I hit send, I made sure my phone was securely zipped into my pocket. It was spring, and we were both dressed comfortably for now, but I knew the temperature would start dropping this afternoon. I hoped my text went through.

I made my way carefully down the rocky slope. There were bushes here and there for me to grab onto. I stopped beside her, holding the base of a small tree.

"Can I see your ankle?" I asked.

She was seated on her hips with one foot propped against a sturdy boulder. She held the other foot up. She had rolled up her pants and loosened her shoe in the time that it had taken me to send that text and scramble down to her. Her ankle was already swelling. I couldn't tell if it was broken, but the swelling concerned me.

"I don't think you should put weight on it."

"I know. It really hurts when I do." She cleared her throat, and I could tell she was trying not to cry.

I curled my arm around her shoulders. "You can cry. If we have to, we'll crawl up. I'll take one step at a time, and you can use your good leg. We'll get you to the top. It's not that far."

She swiped at her tears as she nodded. I shifted to reach my purse, which I'd looped at an angle over my shoulders when we started walking. I found the small bottle of ibuprofen I always kept. "Take this. It will help with the swelling and the pain."

She took those with a few swallows of water from the bottle she carried in her small backpack.

"I texted my brothers. They'll find us." I had faith my brothers would probably all show up.

"Do you think my dad and Uncle Jack will be upset?" Hannah asked.

"No," I said quickly. "Absolutely not."

She blinked and nodded.

"Are you ready to try to move?"

At her nod, I carefully stood and helped her get her balance. Glancing behind us, I was relieved a strip of sandy shoreline was still visible.

We began making our way up the rocky bluff. I knew it was painful for Hannah. She was quiet, but her breath occasionally hissed through her teeth. As soon as we made it to the top, she sat down. The lines on her face were drawn tight, and my heart ached for her. She was clearly in pain.

I sat down beside her in the gravelly flat section of the trail. "We just did the hardest part," I offered encouragingly.

She swiped at the tears rolling down her cheeks and took several breaths. "I know. Let's go."

What had been maybe a half-hour walk in was going to take much longer. I worried about the time and cursed myself for not paying better attention. There was no reply to my text. But the reception had gone from one bar to none. I just prayed my text got through anyway.

As we walked and I tried to support Hannah as best I could, my mind kept detouring to Jack. I missed him, and I knew I loved him. I just didn't know how to make things right. My old doubts were ready and waiting to strike.

Chapter Thirty-Four

JACK

When I got the third call in a row from an unfamiliar number, Derek said, "Fucking answer your phone."

"It's nobody in my contacts. It's probably a scam call."

"Is it local?"

"Yeah, but still. It's an Alaskan area code, but scammers can spoof local numbers," I pointed out.

"Dude, answer your fucking phone."

I intended to ignore him, but the next time it rang, I glanced down to see it was Griffin. I had him in my contacts because we were training together for the hotshot crew.

"Hey man, what's up?"

"Hey, I'm calling because my brother Rhys has been trying to reach you. He got a text from McKenna. I guess she went on a hike with Hannah?"

"Yeah, is that okay?"

"Of course. But Hannah fell and hurt her ankle. McKenna texted Rhys, and we're going to head out and try to meet them. The tide may already be blocking a section of their trail."

I took a quick breath. A sense of panic initially jolted me. But surely, this would be okay?

"Where can I meet you?"

Griffin explained and asked if I would give Derek an update. "Of course." As soon as I hung up, I glanced over. "You know how Hannah asked McKenna to show her that trail?"

"Uh, yeah. We were both there," Derek said dryly.

"Well, Hannah slipped and hurt her ankle. That was Griffin. McKenna texted them about it. They're going to get them."

Derek stood quickly, wobbling a little on his feet.

"You can ride with me, but you're waiting in the car," I said firmly. Derek opened his mouth to argue. I held his gaze. "Seriously?"

"Oh, for fuck's sake, fine. But I'm not sitting here by myself and waiting helplessly. I'll wait in the car helplessly," he muttered.

My brain was ping-ponging dueling concerns as we drove in silence. I was worried about Hannah and McKenna. When we arrived, Rhys, Griffin, and Wyatt waited.

"Derek's staying here," I said.

For all my brother's good attitude about accepting his limitations, he looked beyond annoyed.

"Have you heard anything more?" Derek asked.

Rhys shook his head. "No, and that concerns me."

We began walking with Rhys leading the way. I couldn't even focus on the beautiful view. All I could think about was making sure Hannah and McKenna were okay. I tried to tell myself that I would feel this way about anyone.

My cynicism thought that was a bunch of bullshit. *No, you wouldn't. You miss McKenna every single fucking day.*

We were about fifteen minutes in when Rhys swore. I glanced ahead. "Fuck."

An entire stretch of the trail was closed by the tide lapping against the rocks.

"It's not far through here." Rhys glanced at me. "But getting someone through here with a broken ankle will definitely be a challenge."

Griffin glanced from Rhys to me. "That's why I brought these." He lowered his pack from his shoulders and switched out his leather hiking boots for a pair of tall rubber boots. "I have two pairs," he offered.

Conveniently, he and I wore the same size. Minutes later, we were tromping through the water. I could feel the cold temperature from the water seeping through the boots. Although it was still light out and would be for a few hours, the temperature was dropping.

"I should've known," I said to myself.

"Should've known what?" Griffin asked over his shoulder.

"I should've made sure Hannah had warmer clothes and—"

Griffin stopped in the water, turning to face me. "This isn't a dangerous trail. It's a little rocky in a few spots, but they'll be fine."

He began walking again, and I resumed my ruminations on Hannah and McKenna. I felt a little guilty that I kept worrying about McKenna. But then, I loved her. I needed to figure out what the hell to do about that.

Only a few minutes later, I thought I heard voices ahead. We rounded a bend in the shoreline and stepped onto dry land again. McKenna and Hannah waited on a fallen-down log nearby.

"Jack!" Hannah called, starting to move and stand before McKenna grabbed her by the hand.

"Please wait," McKenna ordered.

They were both clearly okay, and the tension bundled tightly in my shoulders and chest eased up a little. Griffin and I approached, and McKenna looked up. "I thought we had plenty of time before the tide came in, but —"

"I slipped and fell and hurt my ankle," Hannah interjected. "It really slowed us down."

"How much pain are you in?" I asked, kneeling beside Hannah.

"McKenna gave me some ibuprofen, so it's getting better. It really hurt at first. It still hurts if I put any weight on it," Hannah explained.

"Can I take a look?" I asked.

Hannah rolled up her jeans, and Griffin and I checked her ankle. "You'll need an x-ray, but I'm guessing you fractured it."

"Do you think?" Hannah's worried gaze met mine.

"Probably."

"Or a bad sprain," Griffin offered.

"How long do we have to wait for the tide?" Hannah asked.

Griffin grinned. "We're going to carry you."

He glanced toward McKenna. "Your feet will get wet, but it's only a few minutes, and then you'll be able to dry off."

"I can handle it," she replied.

Hannah began apologizing, and the three of us collectively cut her off. "Things happen," I said.

"I'm trying not to be any trouble, though," Hannah said. Her eyes were bright with tears.

"You're not any trouble." I stepped in front of her, kneeling and putting my hands on her shoulders. "Life happens. I promise you don't need to worry about doing life perfectly. Trust me, I fuck up plenty. Slipping and hurting your ankle is what we call an accident."

"I'm a member of the fuckup club," Griffin chimed in.

McKenna glanced among us, offering, "I should've probably realized that we could've come another day when we had more than just a few hours before the tide."

"Are you sure it's okay?" Hannah pressed.

"Absolutely," I said with a firm nod.

Griffin and I got Hannah situated between us with her arms over our shoulders and started walking.

McKenna pointed out, "If she walks ahead of us in the cold water, it would probably bring the swelling down."

Hannah smiled at her, and I was relieved to see her relaxing. I couldn't help but ponder her worries. I thought back to my shock at learning Derek had a daughter and realizing she had no one but him and me to turn to for family. It felt as if her life and ours had spun sideways with the change in a matter of days. Life was a twisty road sometimes. Her presence in our lives only expanded my heart.

Occasionally, I looked ahead at McKenna, gamely tramping through the cold water without hesitation. Maybe I wasn't sure how she felt, but I had missed her. *A lot.* I knew what lay between us was much more than chemistry. I knew I wanted to face the complications instead of avoiding them.

When we got back to the parking lot, we determined Rhys would drive Hannah to the hospital, and we would follow since I had my truck. I didn't want to be separated from Hannah or McKenna even for the short drive to the hospital.

Derek insisted on going with Hannah, which left no room in Rhys's SUV. McKenna ended up riding with me.

On the drive to the hospital, I glanced over. McKenna shivered a little. "You need to change. Let's stop by your place."

"No, I'm fine."

"McKenna, you're cold enough to get hypothermic. We'll meet them at the hospital after you change." I called Griffin, who quickly agreed that was the smart plan.

"Oh my God," she muttered after I ended the call.

"Look, if you show up at the hospital, they'll see you're at risk for hypothermia and maybe keep you for observation. Which option do you want?"

She rolled her eyes. "Fine."

She was still shivering when we got to her place. I suggested she take a shower.

"I don't need a shower," she tried to argue.

"The hot water will warm you up fast."

I wanted to follow her into the shower, but I didn't. Minutes later, she came out. She'd changed into warm, dry clothes and was no longer shivering. She gave me a sheepish smile. "Okay, the shower was smart."

As I stared at her, my heart kicked hard against my ribs, galvanizing me. I crossed the room to stop in front of her. "I've missed you," I said before I could think better of it. "Maybe this isn't what we planned, but I love you. You can tell me you never want a relationship, but I think we have a good thing."

McKenna stared up at me, her eyes wide before she burst into tears.

Chapter Thirty-Five

MCKENNA

I tried to say something, but the only thing that came out was a messy sob.

Jack's worried eyes held mine for a beat before he stepped closer and folded me into his arms. The relief of being held in his strong, protective embrace was so immense that I sobbed harder.

I buried my face in his chest, murmuring between sobs, "I'm sorry I'm freaking out. I never cry like this." That was followed by a hiccup.

He smoothed his hand over my hair and down my back. He simply held me until my sobs stopped.

When I leaned back to look up at him, which took more courage than I wanted to admit, he said, "I certainly didn't mean to make you cry."

I blinked and took a shaky breath. "I miss you too." I scrambled for some courage. "I love you. I didn't mean for that to happen."

Jack's eyes were warm. "I know. Just like I didn't plan to fall in love with you. But here we are. What should we do about it?"

I let my forehead fall to his chest again because I

could hear the steady beat of his heart, and the rhythmic beat soothed me. He smelled good, kind of salty and woodsy and, well, like Jack.

When I looked up again, he brushed my hair away from my forehead, palming my cheeks as he brought his lips to mine. His kiss was soft and lingering. We stood there, our lips barely brushing through several echoing beats of my heart.

"Are you warm?" he asked.

The subtle motion of his words against my own lips sent a wash of heat through me. "Yes," I whispered.

He lifted his head just a fraction and traced his thumb across my bottom lip. "Let's go check on Hannah."

"Will you stay with me tonight?"

My heart raced. Asking that question sent anxiety rushing forward. Even though he had told me he loved me only moments ago, putting that out there elicited a sense of raw vulnerability.

"I was hoping you'd ask," he murmured. He gave me a fierce kiss before stepping back.

Moments later, he insisted I wear a jacket and even wanted me to put a hat on.

I looked askance at him. "I'm fine now," I insisted.

He took a breath, letting it out with a sigh. "Okay."

He reached for my hand across the console of his truck as we drove to the hospital. It felt good to have his hand curled over mine.

We didn't talk on the way over. When we got to the hospital, I glanced over. "I'm sorry."

"For what?" He turned his truck off.

"For not thinking about the tide."

"Sounds like there would've been plenty of time, but Hannah got gimpy."

"I know, but—"

Jack reached over and silenced me with a quick kiss. "You have nothing to apologize for. Now let's go see how Hannah's doing."

We hurried into the hospital. Derek, Rhys, and Griffin were in the waiting area near the emergency room. "She's already had an x-ray. It's a minor fracture," Derek announced.

He looked among us and shook his head as he let out a deep sigh. "For fuck's sake, nobody told me how hard it was to be a father."

Jack gave him a back-slapping hug, and Rhys chuckled, offering, "I get it, man."

We all waited at the hospital until Hannah was discharged. Even though Derek and Jack pointed out that Rhys was not obligated to wait, he insisted it was best for him to drive since his SUV had more space than Jack's truck.

After she came out, a little loopy from some pain meds, and we were all getting situated, she looked from Jack to me. "Don't be stupid. You better stay with McKenna tonight."

My face was on fire. Griffin looked over at me with a lopsided grin. "We all know."

Rhys glanced at Jack. "Just don't make me kick your ass."

———

As soon as we walked into my house, Jack kicked the door shut and spun me around. He caged me between his arms as he stared down at me.

"Buckle up. I need you. Now." His voice verged on a growl as he dipped his head and nibbled lightly on my ear.

Delicious shivers raced over my skin. "I missed you so much," I whispered between kisses.

It started fast, with us tumbling into deep kisses where we couldn't get enough of each other, gasping for breath between and yanking at each other's clothes. Everything slowed down after Jack bundled me into his arms and carried me into the bedroom.

We took our time exploring each other with lazy, sensual kisses. Jack's lips left hot brands on my belly. His fingers stretched me open, bringing me to a sharp climax. I slid my thumb over the precum rolling out of his cock, savoring the salty, earthy flavor of it. His eyes were dark when he laced his fingers with mine and stretched my arms over my head. My legs curled around his hips as he notched himself at my entrance and filled me in a slow, delicious slide. My orgasm reverberated in my bones. I could feel the beat of his heart as he went taut, and his release filled me.

We curled up together, drowsing together on the bed. I didn't want to get up. At all. Ever.

But my stomach growled. Jack chuckled. "Should we get some food?"

I rolled my head to the side, smiling at him. "I think so."

Chapter Thirty-Six

JACK

When I woke the following morning, McKenna was soft and warm beside me with one of her knees thrown over mine. Her fingers traced lazy circles on my chest. I rested my hand over her palm and opened my eyes.

Her eyes met mine. "Are you sure about this?"

I knew what she meant. "Absolutely. I love you."

After we got out of bed, I called Derek to check on Hannah. He reported she was doing great and enjoying the opportunity to order him around and have him get things for her while she rested on the couch.

Hannah insisted on getting on the phone. "How are you doing?" she asked before I could get a word in.

"I think that question should be for you."

"I'm fine. Ibuprofen is more than enough to help with my ankle. I already talked to the school because Dad didn't know he was supposed to call." I could hear her rolling her eyes. I heard Derek in the background pointing out that he didn't know the school protocol. She ignored him. "I'm getting my crutches today, and

I'll go to school tomorrow. Fiona says she can still pick me up and take me to school. How was your night?"

"Uh, fine." I did *not* want to discuss my intimate night with McKenna with my niece.

Her laughter was sly. "You love her, right?" Her tone got serious.

"I do," I said somberly.

"Good. I'm glad you're not being a dumbass anymore."

A few minutes later, McKenna handed me a cup of coffee. "Hannah called me a dumbass," I offered with a grin.

McKenna shrugged. "Teenagers have a powerful bullshit barometer for most adults."

EPILOGUE

Adam Cannon

One year later

I was running late. The story of my fucking life. I rushed through some quarterly reports before running out of the office. McKenna and Jack were having a housewarming at their new house.

I was driving down Main Street when I remembered I had to bring something. "Fuck," I muttered to myself.

My car tires squealed when I turned into the parking lot at the grocery store. I hurried in, dashing to the back deli. I was standing in line when my eyes landed on Tessa Hensen.

Tessa was one of McKenna's closest friends, but I didn't know her all that well. Lately, I'd seen Tessa even more as she was also friends with my new sisters-in-law.

I was pretty sure she thought I was an uptight asshole. If she did, she would be right.

She wore a pair of leggings tucked into fitted

leather boots and a short jacket. I couldn't help but notice that her hips were delectably curvy. When I stepped up to the deli counter beside her and she glanced over, I noticed for the first time that she had thick eyelashes and beautiful brown eyes.

"Oh, hi, Adam," she said, her tone almost dismissive.

That pissed me off. "Hi, Tessa. Good to see you," I added.

She looked over at me again. "Good to see you." She crossed her arms, almost as if she were tucking something around her. "Are you going to the potluck?"

"Yeah. Are you?"

"Of course I am," I replied, my tone sharp.

She turned to face me. With her arms crossed, her breasts plumped up. I suddenly cataloged all kinds of details about Tessa—her tousled auburn curls, slightly lopsided mouth, and full lips.

"You don't always go to family things," Tessa pointed out.

She was right on that count. Everyone in our family was a workaholic, but I was probably the worst.

"Are you actually getting something at the deli for it?" she asked.

"Yeah, isn't that what you're doing?"

"Well, yeah, but my family doesn't own Fireweed Winery. I would've thought maybe..." A pink flush rose on her cheeks.

"You would've thought maybe what?"

"Nothing," she said in a singsong voice.

It was her turn to order, and she got some pasta salad. I ordered next, and we waited. Tessa looked over at me after a few minutes. "You don't have to stand with me."

"Is it a problem that I'm standing with you?" I countered.

I was unable to keep my eyes from dipping down to her breasts briefly before bringing them back up.

"Adam," she ground out.

"What?"

"Were you just checking me out?"

I debated pretending I wasn't, but she had thrown me off balance, and I didn't like it. I figured I might as well see if I could get under her skin. "My apologies. I suppose I was."

Every cell in my body fired when her cheeks flushed a deeper pink. "You're cute."

Even though this brief tit-for-tat started because she got under my skin unintentionally, I meant it. She *was* cute.

TESSA

I tried, I *really* did, not to look at Adam when we were at Jack and McKenna's housewarming potluck. His words played on a loop in my mind. *You're cute.*

Every time I thought about it, I got hot all over. I wasn't supposed to notice McKenna's brother. I hadn't noticed any guy in what seemed like forever. To be specific, not since I started dating my ex-husband. What started off as a mad dash into love turned into possessiveness, jealousy, controlling behavior, and abuse.

I still counted myself lucky that I found a way to get out of that marriage. Even though my ex had ruined me for other men, and not in a good way, I would do it all over again just for my son.

I didn't know if anybody could be more disappointed in me than me, though.

"Tessa?" McKenna prompted.

I glanced over. "Oh! I didn't see you there."

She smiled. "Yeah, I noticed you staring at Adam."

"No, I wasn't," I said quickly. Maybe too quickly.

She grinned. "It's okay if you were."

"Hey, you're the one that broke the pact," I pointed out.

McKenna and I used to have a pact. She wasn't ever going to have a relationship for some reason, and I wasn't because of a really good reason. My aforementioned ex.

She studied me for a moment before she nodded. "I did. So if you change your mind, I'll totally understand. But if it's one of my brothers, say Adam, just spare me the details," she said dryly.

I couldn't help but laugh at that. Jack appeared at McKenna's side, sliding his arm around her waist. He bent low and dusted a kiss on her cheek.

It was just a kiss on her cheek, yet my heart literally ached for a minute. There was a sweetness and an intimacy to the way they were together. Jack was this brawny hotshot firefighter, yet he was so protective and caring with McKenna. He seriously had it bad for her.

I was happy for her, just like I was happy for all my friends falling in love with great guys.

I would never tell them that I secretly worried that maybe they were covering up that things weren't great. That was another shitty thing on the list of shitty things about marrying an abusive man. I had lied to everyone and pretended my life was fine. Even now, nobody really knew how bad it had been.

"What pact?" Jack asked, glancing back and forth between us.

"Tessa and I had a pact. Neither one of us was ever

going to have a relationship. I told you I wasn't into that idea when we met. Remember? No romance, no kids. That was the deal."

Jack's smile was warm as he looked down at her. "I thought the same thing."

"Hey, I am in support of kids," I offered.

McKenna and Jack burst out laughing at that. "We still don't want kids," they said in unison.

"I respect the hell out of that. The world puts a lot of pressure on people to have kids."

"We are going to be the aunts and uncles for anyone who needs one," McKenna explained.

Jack's niece Hannah appeared at his side. "You are the best uncle ever," she said, sliding her hand through his elbow and squeezing.

He grinned down at her, giving her a side hug. "I try."

Derek, Hannah's father, approached. By some freaking miracle, he was still hanging in there. He'd been in cancer treatment for the past year. Even though he was weak, the odds were looking up for him.

"He's a pretty good uncle," Derek said, his tone dry.

"I'm better than pretty good," Jack teased.

Hannah squeezed his elbow again. "You're the best, Uncle Jack."

I was still smiling a few minutes later when I slipped down the hallway to go to the bathroom off McKenna's study.

That door was closed, so I leaned against the wall and waited. A moment later, it opened, and Adam stepped out. The second I saw him, my pulse shot off like a rocket.

Adam stopped in front of me. We studied each

other. Objectively speaking, Adam was handsome. He had dark hair paired with blue-gray eyes. He was tall with broad shoulders.

My pulse raced along, and wave after wave of heat rolled through me.

"I stand by my observation," he finally said, his voice all low and rumbly.

"What?" My voice sounded breathy, which was ridiculous. I literally couldn't think. I didn't even know what he was talking about.

"You're cute," he said, his voice dropping an octave lower. "You're also sexy."

My pussy actually clenched. Suddenly, I wanted to kiss him. But there were no kisses in my life.

He lifted a hand, and his knuckles brushed along my cheek.

The air felt lit with a charge. "I want to kiss you."

I was about to open my mouth and say, "Please do," but then he said, "I'm not going to because I think I know what happened."

"What do you mean?"

Adam was quiet for several beats. I didn't know where this feeling came from, but I felt an intense sense of protectiveness emanating from him. "When I saw you earlier, I wondered why you're kind of prickly. But then I remembered you were married to Rich. I knew him in high school before you dated him. He was a controlling asshole to his girlfriend back then."

I blinked. My heart raced, and not in a good way. I swallowed nervously because I remembered Rich talking about his high school girlfriend. He'd said she was a "fucking bitch" and that she'd cheated on him.

As if he could read my mind, Adam said, "She never cheated on him. He was just a controlling jerk. I imagine he was with you too. Guys like that don't usually change."

All I could do was stare at Adam.

"Maybe I shouldn't have said that," he added, his tone laced with a gentleness that cracked the edges of my hardened heart.

I shrugged. "It's okay." My voice was barely above a whisper.

His fingers trailed down my neck, and I still wasn't afraid. "Maybe another time. If you want to kiss me, let me know."

I felt bereft when Adam stepped back from me. He pressed two fingers against his lips and blew me a kiss before walking out of the room.

My knees were liquid. I had no idea how I walked into the bathroom, but I did. It was all I could do not to chase him.

Late that night, long after I went home, I texted McKenna. *Do you happen to have Adam's number?*

Thank you for reading Jack & McKenna's story! Want a glimpse of the future for them? Join my newsletter to receive an exclusive scene.

Sign up here: https://BookHip.com/SVAJKLM

p.s. If you are already subscribed, you'll still be able to access the scene.

Up next in the Fireweed Harbor Series is Wait
For You!

Adam & Tessa never noticed each other before. Until
one night and one almost-kiss.

Adam promises Tessa a kiss. If, and *only if*, she
wants one.

Tessa most definitely isn't looking for love, but a kiss
seems harmless enough. She has a messy, painful past
and just wants some peace in her life. Not romance.
Until grumpy Adam just might make her want it all.

Don't miss Adam & Tessa's swoony, hot and intense
romance!

One click to pre-order: Wait For You - due out June
2024!

For more swoony romance...

This Crazy Love kicks off the Swoon Series - small
town southern romance with enough heat to melt you!
Jackson & Shay's story is epic - swoon-worthy &
intensely emotional. Jackson just happens to be Shay's
brother's best friend. He's also *seriously* easy on the
eyes. Shay has a past, the kind of past she would most
definitely like to forget. Past or not, Jackson is about
to rock her world. Don't miss their story!

Burn For Me is a second chance romance for the ages.
Sexy firefighters? Check. Rugged men? Check.
Wrapped up together? Check. Brave the fire in this
hot, small-town romance. Amelia & Cade were high
school sweethearts & then it all fell apart. When they
cross paths again, it's epic - don't miss Cade's story!

For more small town romance, take a visit to Last
Frontier Lodge in Diamond Creek. A sexy, alpha SEAL
meets his match with a brainy heroine in Take Me

Home. Marley is all brains & Gage is all brawn. Sparks fly when their worlds collide. Don't miss Gage & Marley's story!

If sports romance lights your spark, check out The Play. Liam is a British footballer who falls for Olivia, his doctor. A twist of forbidden heats up this swoon-worthy & laugh-out-loud romance. Don't miss Liam & Olivia's story.

FIND MY BOOKS

Thank you for reading One More Time! I hope you enjoyed the story. If so, you can help other readers find my books in a variety of ways.

1) Write a review!
2) Sign up for my newsletter, so you can receive information about upcoming new releases & receive a FREE copy of one of my books: http://jhcroixauthor. com/subscribe/
3) Like and follow my Amazon Author page at https:// amazon.com/author/jhcroix
4) Follow me on Bookbub at https://www.bookbub. com/authors/j-h-croix
5) Follow me on Instagram at https://www.instagram. com/jhcroix/
6) Like my Facebook page at https://www.facebook. com/jhcroix

Fireweed Harbor Series

Make You Mine

Dare To Fall

Be The One

One More Time

Wait For You - due out June 2024!

Ever After All - due out August 2024!

Light My Fire Series

Wild With You

Hold Me Now

Only Ever Us

Fall For Me

Keep Me Close

With Every Breath

All It Takes

Take Me Now

Meant To Be

Dare With Me Series

Crash Into You

Evers & Afters

Come To Me

Back To Us

Take Me There

After We Fall

Swoon Series

This Crazy Love

Wait For Me

Break My Fall

Truly Madly Mine

Still Go Crazy

If We Dare

Steal My Heart

Into The Fire Series

Burn For Me

Slow Burn

Burn So Bad
Hot Mess
Burn So Good
Sweet Fire
Play With Fire
Melt With You
Burn For You
Crash & Burn
That Snowy Night
Brit Boys Sports Romance
The Play
Big Win
Out Of Bounds
Play Me
Naughty Wish
Diamond Creek Alaska Novels
When Love Comes
Follow Love
Love Unbroken
Love Untamed
Tumble Into Love
Christmas Nights
Lodge Series
Take Me Home
Love at Last
Just This Once
Falling Fast
Stay With Me
When We Fall
Hold Me Close
Crazy For You
Just Us

ACKNOWLEDGMENTS

Gestures broadly to all the readers in the world -
THANK YOU!
xoxo
J.H. Croix